M000190205

WOULDN'T YOU LOVE TO LOVE HER

SHANNON JUMP

Copyright © 2022 by Shannon Jump
All rights reserved.

No part of this publication may be reproduced, stored or transmitted in any
form or by any means, electronic, mechanical, photocopying, recording,
scanning, or otherwise without written permission from the publisher. It is
illegal to copy this book, post it to a website, or distribute it by any other
means without permission.

This novel is entirely a work of fiction. The names, characters and incidents
portrayed in it are the work of the author's imagination. Any resemblance to
actual persons, living or dead, events or localities is entirely coincidental.

Designations used by companies to distinguish their products are often
claimed as trademarks. All brand names and product names used in this
book and on its cover are trade names, service marks, trademarks and
registered trademarks of their respective owners. The publishers and the
book are not associated with any product or vendor mentioned in this book.
None of the companies referenced within the book have endorsed the book.

Copy Editing by Librum Artis Editorial Services

First edition published March 2022
ISBN: 978-0-578-34329-7 (Paperback)
ASIN: B09NGK2B7K(Kindle Edition)

ALSO BY SHANNON JUMP

<u>Contemporary Fiction</u>

My Only Sunshine

<u>Psychological Suspense Thriller</u>

Even Though It's Breaking

<u>The *Crimes of Passion* Psychological Thriller Series</u>

Wouldn't You Love to Love Her

CONTENT WARNING

This book is intended for readers over the age of eighteen and contains mature content unsuitable for younger audiences. For a full list of warnings, please contact the author at info@shannonjumpwritesbooks.com.

For Mom

(But seriously, please don't read this.)

She kissed me.
She kissed the devil.
Only a ***beautiful*** soul
like hers would kiss the damned.

— DANIEL SAINT

ALLEGEDLY, OF COURSE

Alisha

THERE'S a stain on the wall to my right. It's a dull brown that I imagine, when fresh, was once a bright shade of red. It's low enough to the ground that had I not been lying here on the concrete floor, I might never have noticed it. I stare at it now, the stain, my head turned sharply to the side, arms folded across my stomach. It's faint against the cream-colored brick wall, no bigger than the size of a pea, the edges almost jagged.

A cast-off droplet.

It's definitely blood, and probably a direct correlation to the reason I don't have a cellmate. Rumor has it my predecessor, and former inmate of cell number 154, slit her own throat with a shiv fashioned from her toothbrush.

The shiv? Currently missing in action.

I shudder at the thought, my stomach churning as I consider the amount of pressure she would need to apply to create a fatal wound like that from a piece of plastic—on her own neck, no less. Goosebumps prickle my skin, and I'm faced again with the reality that this isn't a dream. That I am, in fact, awake, locked behind a set of metal bars. A prisoner of the state.

This is my new normal.

I won't be waking up tomorrow in the comfort of my own bed, my husband snoring softly beside me as I roll over to watch him sleep. I picture his handsome face, the prominent features I've always found endearing: the tiny scar above his right eye, punctuated by a faint set of crow's feet that he always swore weren't there. The chiseled jaw, lined with prickly stubble. His head full of dark hair that I loved to run my fingers through, often disheveled from a good night's sleep. The necessary rise and fall of his chest that tells me he's alive will not be there.

A tear slides down my cheek and catches me by surprise. I want to wipe it away, but don't. I leave it there for him in case he needs it, in case he's watching.

It's proof, somehow, that I feel things, too.

Not that anyone seems to believe it. I suppose I can't blame them; it's not like I've given them much reason to. The one and only thing they think they know about me isn't something I'm particularly proud of, but what can I do?

It is the popular opinion of many that I killed my husband.

The media has a lot to do with that.

I suppose the evidence against me does as well.

That's why I've spent the last ninety-three days locked in a tiny concrete cell that on a good day reeks of urine and weeks-old body odor. Most days it's mixed with the faint scent of blood, as if it's been shed in large quantities, only to be wiped away with nothing more than cheap, unscented bar soap and lukewarm water, sure to linger indefinitely.

On the worst of days it reeks of old socks. Of sex. And sweat. And sour breath. Some of the women here seem to love it, though. Me? I don't think I'll ever get used to the stench of this place.

No sane person could.

These women...they're damaged goods. Most of them are unapologetic criminals lined up and begging for their chance at a sexual encounter with a certain corrections officer who'll go home to his loving wife and brood of children immediately afterward—as if he's done nothing wrong.

I'll be here, in this hell-hole, until my trial begins next week. At least I think it's next week; all the days have blurred together at this point. For someone like me who sticks to their cell most of the time, there's not much to break up the monotony.

Although I do get quite a bit of fan mail these days. And as if it weren't an invasion of privacy—because there's no such thing as privacy here in prison—each piece is carefully inspected, read, and analyzed by some *qualified* personnel. I don't need to mention the fact that such an act is highly illegal outside of these walls, a federal offense punishable by imprisonment, actually.

Oh, the irony.

But here? Mail is a privilege that must be earned.

Not that it matters—the one person I expected to hear from has yet to reach out, not that I blame them. And it's not like I'd care to talk to a cellmate to pass the time—if I had one. Isn't that jail house 101—not to speak with other inmates as you await trial? I'm pretty sure that's what I've always heard on those Thursday night drama shows. It's fine, though. I prefer it this way, really I do.

I can't imagine I'd make a decent friend in here even if I tried.

"Thompson, Alisha!" bellows the CO from the other side of my cell. He's not one of us—a caged animal—no, he's free to roam as he pleases. I think of him more as our lion tamer, the man responsible for this circus we're all unwillingly performing in.

He owns us.

All of us.

I'm not sure he understands he's not supposed to get high on his own supply, but he hasn't been caught with his pants down yet, and none of us have bothered to report him. So, the cycle continues; the show goes on.

Not that it matters.

He's one of the most decorated guards here, Officer Joshua Marshall.

"Present," I announce sullenly, my eyes still locked in on the shit-colored bloodstain. I hear his feet shuffle, his heavy boots dragging in the dirt that litters the floors around here. He clears his throat and taps his pen on the metal bars that protect me from the general population for over twelve hours a day.

Or them from me.

"What are you doing on the floor?" he hisses, his voice softer than the usual boom that reverberates from his throat.

"Sunbathing."

"Bullshit. What are you doing on the floor, Thompson?" he asks again, a bit more gruffly this time.

I stare blankly at the stain, focused in deep concentration. I refuse to look at him.

He likes to see the fear in our eyes.

But fear is nothing but a useless emotion, an unnecessary burden I'd rather not carry.

"Thompson!" he barks, his voice echoing in the hollow space. I shudder and finally relax—as much as one possibly can on a concrete floor—and the warmth quickly spreads through my lower extremities. It's brazened and unpleasant, the urine, as it soaks through my pale gray jumpsuit and onto the floor beneath me.

I held it in all day for this.

"What the *fuck*?" Officer Marshall says, disgust riddled across his face. "Clean it up!" He shakes his head and backs away, sighing as he makes a mark on his clipboard and moves on with his head count.

"Thorson, Francis!"

Once he's far enough down the row, I peel myself from the dank floor and strip out of my prison-issued scrubs—parts of them now a darker shade of gray, parts of them sticking to my body in ways I'd rather not think about. I toss them into the hobbit-sized sink next to my toilet before stripping the sheet from the twin mattress and wrapping it around myself like a bath towel. I yell for the other CO, the female one— Officer Marin—that will bring me fresh clothes, even though she'll mutter to herself about my inability to use the toilet. She's quite fed up with my lack of personal hygiene these days, so she tells me.

But I can't expect her to understand, not in her current state of oblivion.

Officer Marshall can do no wrong.

Obviously, I can use the toilet just fine, especially seeing as I've been awarded with my own personal commode not even five feet from the head of my bed. The thing is, I'd rather piss myself once a day than engage in another romp session with a certain CO who can't keep his dick in his pants.

See, showers are another thing that's privileged here. An

inmate is not guaranteed a shower just because they pee their pants.

It does, however, make me much less desirable.

Which means I get to spend the night lying on top of a thin plastic mattress, wondering where the hell things went wrong instead of getting pounded up against a brick wall.

So, I piss myself.

It's rancid, yes, but sometimes it's the best thing I smell all day.

It is my unpopular opinion that Officer Marshall belongs six feet under alongside my husband, but that's a topic for another day.

My name is Alisha Renee Thompson, inmate number 090285, and I am awaiting trial for the premeditated murder of my husband.

Allegedly, of course.

MONOLOGUES, MELTDOWNS, & MURDER

THE VIRGINITY MONOLOGUE

Alisha

I SHOULD GO BACK to the beginning, maybe tell you a little more about myself and why I'm here. Your confusion will otherwise get the best of you, and we certainly can't have that.

Let me start with a cold, hard truth, and say this: you will either love me or you will hate me. You may even love to hate me. There is no in between, no mutual understanding we can come to—even as the mature adults we are. There's no agreeing to disagree, no acceptance of opposing positions. The truth is, most people don't like me, and the ones who do are either lying to themselves or just as fucked up in the head as I am. That, or they want to sleep with me, and once they do they usually hate me afterward, so the outcome is generally the same.

This brings me back to my original point: the odds that you'll like me are not great.

I get it; it happens all the time. I don't sugarcoat a damn thing and sometimes people take offense to the half-witted shit that spews from my mouth. I won't filter my thoughts or censor my language just to make you feel better, so you'll have to get used to it or start heading for the door.

Now, let's get one more thing out on the table, shall we? I'm a sex addict. You may be a bit confused by that fact, considering my lack of interest in Officer Marshall's advances, but it's true. Of course, I blatantly denied it for years, but as of late I've really come to terms with this society-plagued, deviant-like addiction of mine. You're probably wondering how I *manage* it.

Well, in truth, I don't. Or at least didn't. Things are different now—by necessity—but for most of my adult life, I did nothing to minimize my addiction and everything to capitalize on it.

How? Well, have you ever heard of a little thing called adult streaming services? Live webcam girls? Of course you have; I don't even know why I'm asking, but whether you openly admit it or not, you've probably indulged in adult entertainment at least once in your life. Perhaps you've ventured out to a strip club, or fancied yourself a lap dance or two. You may have even dabbled in the anonymity of porn, perhaps all by your lonesome, or in the privacy of the bedroom you share with your better half. Seriously, don't kid yourself, we've all taken a peek behind the proverbial curtain.

But, we're not here to discuss *your* sexual habits, we're here to discuss *mine*, as much as I'd rather not. That adult streaming service I mentioned? It's what I do to earn a living, how I pay my bills. I run a livestream channel of adults-only content that subscribers can access for the low price of $19.95 per hour. On a slow day, I average about twenty-five-hundred viewers per hour, three days a week, three hours each day. That's it. Easy peasy, lemon frickin' squeezy.

Pretty lucrative, right? Go ahead and do that math, because once I tell you what I do on that live channel, you'll not only envy me for my money, you'll also be right back to hating me. To that I say *to each their own.*

My streaming channel is called Lisha's Bedroom. That probably tells you all you need to know, but just in case your engine is a little slow on the intake today, I'll make it a little more clear for you. Essentially, I'm a glorified stripper. But from the comfort of my own home, sans the lap dances and uninvited groping.

Plus, I get to play with toys, and nobody yells at me when I don't put them away.

The money obviously speaks for itself—and yes, I even pay my taxes like a good girl. That said, you'll wonder a few things about me as you get to know me against my will. Like why I live in a less-than-average sized house across the street from the trailer park where I grew up, even though I can (clearly) afford much better. Or why I sound like I don't give a shit half the time. Spoiler alert: I don't.

And through it all, you'll picture the man I've been accused of killing, and you'll wonder what the hell he was doing with a woman like me in the first place. You'll probably even use a few derogatory names at my expense.

It's okay, I'm not mad. People questioned my relationship with my husband long before he ended up dead, so it's nothing new. Hell, even I did from time to time. Anyway, now that I've gotten a few things off my chest, let me tell you how I ended up in the Smithson Women's Penitentiary, awaiting trial for his murder.

You may still hate me by the end of this; you were practically destined to by default. And that's fine. Or, you may surprise us all and come out loving me a little more than you already did, in which case be prepared for your friends to judge you and start asking questions about your sanity. Like I said, there's not really a middle ground for us here.

I'll start from what I consider the beginning—this may take a while, so bear with me.

I've always loved sex.

It's no secret to anyone who knows me, and I stopped giving a shit about that fact a long time ago. As a woman, sex is one of those taboo subjects we're not really supposed to talk about—even though our lovers tend not to complain behind closed doors when the freak comes out at night, right?

I digress.

Basically, you're a slut if you give it up too easily, a whore if you sleep around, and a prude if you're still a virgin after the age of eighteen. I've been called all but the latter.

I've also been called worse.

It changes nothing for me in the long run. I couldn't give two shits what someone else thinks of me. Most of the time, anyway. And I've always had a small circle of friends—often nonexistent, if I'm being honest. A partial hazard of my upbringing, but mostly due to my chosen career, which I came to terms with a long time ago.

But with sex I'm always in control. I can be whoever I want to be—or whoever *they* want me to be. That's a liberating power. It's just as addicting as any drug or the strongest proof alcohol.

As a teen, I had explored my own body quite extensively before I ever gave my V-card to anyone, and as a result, I knew what I liked at an early age. I was comfortable in my own skin before most girls even learned what a clitoris was. I could even say that word without blushing.

I made the mistake of mentioning all of this to my therapist, Kristin. We went on discussing it for seven years and still don't see eye-to-eye on the topic.

Personally, I don't think she understands what she's missing.

"There are rehabilitation centers that specialize in sex addiction," she told me during one of our first sessions together. I was taken aback, unsure how admitting one's love for sex could immediately result in a recommendation for rehab, but apparently she was going down that road and dragging me along for the ride.

"I'm not a sex addict," I argued, now on the defense.

"With all due respect, Alisha, I have to admit that I think you might be." She scribbled a note on the legal pad that rested in her lap.

"I just really love sex," I told her. She made another notation on the page and then adjusted her glasses, the thick plastic frames almost too large for her slim face.

"I think we should explore that statement."

"Why?" I asked. At this point, I leaned back on the obligatory couch, crossed my legs and folded my arms over my chest. I was making a point and therefore felt the need to convey that point with stereotypical body language. I immediately wondered what notation she might make at such childish behavior, but that didn't stop me from doing it.

"How often do you have sex?" she asked, looking at me expectantly.

At that moment, I debated ghosting her, maybe telling her to fuck off and mind her own damn business, but then I remembered that *technically* I *was* her business. I mean, I was paying her to give a shit, to ask the uncomfortable questions. So, I sucked it up and answered her question.

"On a good month? Every day. But, that's only if I'm seeing…" I paused, unsure which pronoun to use to finish the statement. "…someone," I finished, punctuating the sentence with a nod of my head.

"And, when you are seeing *someone*, is this someone you are exclusive with?"

I knew where she was going with the line of questioning; I sensed the tone in her voice. The judgment and overall condescension. "I've been known to be a bit promiscuous," I admitted, reluctantly so.

"Mm-hm," she said, her pen scribbling again. It was silent as she jotted her notes, and I uncrossed my legs before leaning forward and resting my elbows on my knees. I was certain she had flinched, but I couldn't imagine why, it wasn't like I had threatened her.

"Just say it," I snapped. Kristin looked at me apologetically, almost like she felt sorry for me.

"Alisha, I believe you have some unhealthy sexual habits."

"You have *got* to be kidding me," I said, jumping to my feet. I didn't need her ridicule and refused to sit through it any longer. Grabbing my purse and tucking it under my armpit, I waved an aggressive finger in her general direction. "Maybe *you* have some unhealthy sexual habits," I hissed. "Try getting laid sometime, maybe it'll help you pull the stick out of your ass."

I walked over to the door, prepared to make a clean exit from the chamber of hell, my hand resting on the knob. "And you know what? I don't appreciate you slut-shaming me." I huffed and puffed my way out the door, making sure to slam it nice and hard before rushing past the patrons who waited their turn in the lobby.

Despite my dramatic exit that day, since I already had the appointment on my calendar, I returned to see Kristin the following week. Apparently, I wasn't getting off—so to speak —that easily in the shrink department.

With neither of us offering apologies, Kristin picked the conversation up right where it left off. She asked the dreaded question I had seen coming, the one that subconsciously caused me to throw a tantrum and walk out of there in the first place—it's not a story I tell people, not even my late husband.

"How did you lose your virginity, Alisha?"

I decided in that moment to be *extra* diligent in answering Kristin's questions going forward. In fact, I made sure to elaborate, sharing in great detail, about the afternoon I was officially deflowered. The story goes a little something like this:

I bid adieu to my virginity back in 2002, at the age of seventeen—a little late in the game in comparison to my peers at the time, honestly. That virginal gift, in all its entirety, went to Brandon Gould, the hunky star quarterback on the varsity football team. Not that we had ever uttered a word to one another, but I'd seen him checking me out in the halls in between classes, watched him stare at my cleavage from across the lunchroom. He was dating Amy Silverton, the head cheerleader—because, of course he was, right?—so technically he wasn't *supposed* to be checking out other girls. They'd been an item since junior year and according to the rumor mill, she had yet to put out.

Poor guy.

I ran into him at the Tom Thumb gas station one afternoon after school. I had stopped in for a Milky Way bar. Brandon stood behind me at the register, a Snickers and a bottle of pop in his hand.

"I'll get that," he said, placing his items on the counter next to my highly superior Milky Way. We made eye contact as he pulled his wallet out of his back pocket—Velcro, which almost made me laugh; I wouldn't have pegged him for a Velcro wallet kind of guy.

For some reason, I found myself wondering what Brandon's dick looked like. *Is it big? Is he circumcised?* I inadvertently undressed him with my eyes while he paid for our candy bars. This was a habit I'd picked up recently, one I couldn't seem to turn off no matter how hard I tried. I often walked through the halls at school wondering how big all the boys' dicks were and whether or not they were circumcised.

I'm telling you, I don't know how men do it, because I would have been walking around pitching a tent everywhere I went if I had a penis. At least as a woman I could hide my arousal from prying eyes.

"Thank you," I said to Brandon when he handed a five-dollar bill to the cashier, a ginger with several odd-shaped freckles across his nose.

"It's no problem."

The cashier, Allen—according to his worn-out name tag —slid the change across the counter and watched us stand there awkwardly. "Get a room," he mumbled before turning away.

We left the store, me in front, Brandon behind me and likely checking out my ass, which was rounding out nicely thanks to the squats I'd been doing in gym class. I made sure to adjust my V-neck enough to display a little extra of the cleavage I knew he'd been admiring, too. I turned and thanked him again for the candy bar, waving with it in my hand as I grabbed the bike I'd left leaning against the side of the building.

"Do you need a ride?" he offered, motioning toward his single cab pickup.

"Oh. That'd be great, thanks."

He opened the tailgate and slid my bike into the bed while I hopped into the passenger seat. I was surprised to find the cab was relatively clean. Most guys that offered rides didn't keep such a clean vehicle.

"Where do you live?" he asked, buckling his seatbelt. I fastened mine as well, making sure it hugged my chest and further accentuated my breasts, which you've probably figured out by now had developed quite nicely.

Brandon cleared his throat and diverted his eyes forward.

"Just over by Lake Pulaski," I said. *In the trailer park, I left out.*

"You're, um...very pretty." Brandon managed. I pretended to blush and gave him my best version of bedroom eyes. "You're a junior, right?" he asked.

"Yep."

"I've seen you around school. Alisha, is it?" he asked, but pronouncing it "Uh-lish-uh."

"It's Alisha...like A-leesh-uh, but with an 'sh' instead of a 'c.' It's spelled differently," I corrected.

"I like it," he admitted with a coy smile.

"This is me," I said, pointing to the blue rambler on the corner. He pulled up to the curb and put the truck in park, but made no movement to open his door. Neither did I.

"I'm going to break up with Amy," he blurted.

"Oh."

"She's, uh, not my type. Not really, anyway."

"I thought all the star quarterbacks were supposed to date the head cheerleaders?" I teased.

He laughed. "Well, in this case, the head cheerleader is kind of stuck-up."

"Oh..." I said again. We sat in silence for another beat, and I wasn't sure if I should get out or stay. Brandon shimmied out of his letterman's jacket and draped it over the back of the seat before planting his hand on my thigh—sending an unexpected shiver through my entire body.

I'd never had a boyfriend, although I'd made out with a couple guys under the bleachers at football games before. But Brandon's touch was electric, pulsing. It had taken me by surprise.

"I really like you," he said, his hand snaking further up my thigh. I inhaled a breath and unbuckled my seatbelt so I could slide over next to him.

"You do?" I asked, somewhat seductively like I'd heard the women do in the porn DVDs I'd stolen from one of my mom's boyfriends.

"Yes." He swallowed the lump in his throat. I leaned back in the seat and spread my legs. I couldn't help but watch his face; he was mesmerized by my forwardness, his eyes dilated and his mouth slightly open while his tongue traced his bottom lip. When he didn't move his hand, I placed mine over the top of it and guided him to the wetness inside my skirt. I hadn't dressed appropriately for the fall weather, but it was suddenly worth having been cold all day.

"How much?" I asked.

"So much," he said before he leaned over and kissed me. His lips were soft and his tongue rough as it plunged into my mouth.

"Not here," I said, breaking the kiss. He adjusted himself in the seat, his bulge prominent in his track pants.

He drove us to an abandoned farm on the other side of the lake, and as soon as he pulled onto the gravel road, I unbuckled my seatbelt and lifted my shirt over my head. His hands were on me before he even had the truck in park, and it inadvertently rolled forward a bit.

"Sorry," he said nervously, tapping the brake and shifting into the proper gear. I reached behind me and unclasped my bra, admiring his face while he watched my breasts tumble out.

His mouth dropped, his eyes opening wide, but he said nothing. It was clearly his first time seeing boobs in the flesh.

He slid his pants and boxers down and they fell to his ankles, bunching in a heap at his feet on the dirty floor mat. He was already hard, and I gasped in excitement at the sight of him because I figured he would like that—it's what all the porn stars seemed to do, anyway. Like they'd been given a gift and couldn't contain their excitement.

"Put your mouth on it," he coached, his hand on the back of my head to draw me closer. I took him in my mouth, and the sound of his moans filled the cab of the truck. Something had come over me in that moment, and I had never felt so alive, like I possessed some sort of magical power over him.

I climbed on his lap, still very much in control, and while the whole act of sex took less than ten minutes from start to finish, when I felt his release inside me, I silently cheered for myself. I was proud of my newfound abilities, at the fact that I'd gotten him off.

Afterward, he shucked the condom out the window and then drove me home—or at least, he thought he did. I told him I lived in the blue rambler we'd pulled up to earlier, but I actually lived in the trailer pack across the street. The blue rambler belonged to Gretta Maylen, the sweet older lady whose dog I let out every day after school for ten bucks a week.

What makes this loss of virginity extra pathetic is that Brandon never did break things off with Amy. When I asked him about it under the bleachers later that week while giving him a blow job, he said they'd worked things out and that he'd deny it if I ever told anyone what happened between us. That he wasn't going to let a *girl like me* ruin a good thing.

As if it were my fault he had just cheated on his girlfriend.

After he came, I wiped his secretions off my mouth, stood up, and spit the mouthful back in his face. Before he had a chance to realize his own semen was dripping down his cheek, I shoved my tits back into my top, flipped him the bird, and sashayed my way out of there.

I'd learned the nasty truth about guys that week: they'll use a woman for her body just because they *can*, and then go home to their girlfriend, wife, or lover afterward without a pang of guilt.

And the worst thing anyone ever calls them is a player; they may even get a high five or two.

This is why I love sex, you see? Because the first guy I ever let fuck me managed to do so in more ways than one. But he taught me a valuable lesson, too. I decided that day that I'd never let another guy like Brandon use me again. That I would always be the one who would determine whether sex was a game or an act of endearment.

And I've been playing that game ever since.

THE MOST PERFECT SPECIMEN

Alisha

GROWING up in a rundown trailer park was about what you'd expect. It was dirty, shady, and at times, a little unsettling. Our front door never locked properly, so one day, since my mother was too much of a junkie to do it herself, I used twenty dollars of my dog-sitting money to buy one of those locks you screw into the top of the door—I figured even if an intruder could break the door off the hinges, at least the cheap lock would give me a chance to get out of there before they managed to get inside.

I was becoming more resourceful, too, so when I got home I asked our twenty-something neighbor, Cole, to install the lock for me, even though I could have done it myself. Cole, being the nice guy that he was, didn't charge anything for it, and I felt bad, so I sucked him off as a thank you. It kind of became a thing for us after that; he'd help out around the trailer when my mom was gone on a bender, and I'd thank him with blow jobs.

And, I guess it sounds a bit ludicrous, looking back, but after my virginity-stripping romp in Brandon's pickup, I learned that sex could be a useful tool for a girl like me.

I knew I was pretty.

I knew I was well endowed in the chest region.

So why not use those things to my advantage? I didn't have much else going for me, so yes, I slept around quite a bit and was what you might refer to as a closet ho. I made my rounds through the guys in school but was never actually labeled a whore because none of their other halves ever found out. And the guys didn't talk; it was like they had some secret bro code, and they all knew about it. It worked out well for me; I got to get my jollies off and the guys whose girlfriends wouldn't put out—or did, but lacked a sense of adventure— got to stay in their idealistic high school romances but still get their dicks wet every once in a while.

I would've charged for my services had such a thing been legal. I've never quite understood how it's okay for a porn star to make money having sex just because they're consid- ered "actors," yet it's prostitution if you charge for it from the comfort of your own home, sans the camera.

I considered getting into porn, to be honest. Why not make some money doing what I loved most? I had been blessed with the body for it, even though I rarely exercised and never had the money to eat healthily. And while stereo- typically, most guys really do prefer blondes, it turns out they're also suckers for a blue-eyed brunette with thick lips and loose morals.

In college, I let a guy film me while I sucked him off. I didn't know his name, but he was drunk, and while I was ready and willing to give him the best blow job he'd ever had

—for the sake of the camera, of course—the asshole couldn't keep it up, and because of that, my amateur porn debut never made it to the internet.

Anyway, I digress. Kristin says I'm a walking, talking cliche with this shit. I asked her what she meant by that, even though I knew the answer, and she back-pedaled pretty aggressively. I moved on and pretended to forgive her, but mentally I added another derogatory mark to her Yelp review.

College got more exciting once word got around that I wasn't afraid to put my sexuality to use. Eventually, I was invited to just about every party on campus, and they were *insane*, to say the least. Since I didn't drink, these parties were merely an easy way for me to experiment sexually, and just about everyone was fair game. I didn't know a single "happy" couple who didn't sleep around behind their partner's back. And they had a knack for spilling the dirt on each other, too. It's amazing what you can find out about relationships when you're lying around letting the after-sex glow wear off. Guys talk more than you'd think, and it's almost unsettling when they share their dark fantasies with you *after* you've already let them stick their dick in you. Like, thanks, asshole. Thanks for letting me know that you're a fucking creep *after* I got you off.

I started screening men a little differently after college, and while I still had my fair share of weirdos, they were fewer and further between.

But it wasn't just men that propositioned me for sex; the women were equally as horny and just as unfaithful. I tried to draw the line somewhere, though. There were enough men around campus that I didn't need to take advantage of the women, too. I hated to be a snob, but other than letting a couple girls go down on me, I enjoyed the dick too much to formally cross over. I wasn't sure what that said about my sexuality, but I also didn't care to put a label on it either.

Now, I know I claimed early on that my sex life wasn't an addiction, but these days, I'll be the first to admit that it is. And I've always had an intense addiction to porn. I couldn't get enough of it—and sometimes I watched it only for research purposes, figuring I could learn a few things from it.

And that's exactly what I was doing on that Saturday afternoon in 2015 when I first laid eyes on Dylan Thompson.

I lived alone in a one-bedroom apartment—with a sex "addiction" like mine, coupled with my habit of walking around naked, and the need to work from home, how could I *not* live alone? I had just finished getting off to some amateur porn when there was a knock at my door. I stilled, buck naked on the couch, and silently listened for a second knock. Non-residents did have a tendency to show up at the wrong apartments.

Knock, knock.

"Fuck," I mumbled under my breath. I slid my arms through my kimono robe and wrapped the fabric around my torso. "Who is it?" I yelled through the peephole-less door.

"Uh, hi. It's Dylan," the stranger answered.

"I don't know any Dylans," I said with a huff.

"Gretta Maylen's grandson? I called the other day…"

Oh fuck.

Fuck. Fuck. Fuck. I had completely forgotten he would be stopping by. Mrs. Maylen had moved into a nursing home the week prior, and her grandson, a Realtor, had cleaned out her house to get it ready to put up for sale. He'd called and said she'd left something for me and asked if he could come by. I had no idea what she could have possibly left for me, but I had agreed and given him my address. In all my years living across the street from Mrs. Maylen and watching her beloved goldendoodle, I'd never met her grandson.

I unhooked the chain from the top of the door, flipped the deadbolt and pulled the door open. There before me was the sexiest and most perfect specimen of a man I'd ever seen in my entire life.

"Oh. Um. Hi," he said. He scratched his head of beautiful brown hair and his equally beautiful brown eyes trailed up and down my body before settling on something behind me.

"Hi," I said, slowly turning around to see what he was looking at so intently.

The porn.

I forgot to shut off the fucking porn.

"Oh, my God! I'm *so* sorry! One second!" I lunged frantically away from the door, hopping over the back of the couch, and snatching up the TV remote. Never before had I jammed my finger so hard into the power button. My habit of watching on mute—on account of the painfully fake sounds that erupted from some of those women—had backfired. I stood motionless for a moment, unsure if he'd be standing there when I turned back around.

He was.

Still beautiful as ever.

"I see I've interrupted you." He pointed to my ensemble, and it was at this time that I remembered I was only wearing a silk kimono robe. It was another second later that I realized I'd never actually tied the belt of that kimono robe, and it had flown open in my haste to turn off the porn, putting all my lady bits on full display to the gorgeous stranger at my door.

I grabbed at the robe and pulled it back over my body, holding it closed with my arms since I wasn't sure where the belt had disappeared to.

"I'm having a rough day," I admitted. He laughed, and it

was the most incredible laugh I've ever heard, throaty and full of bass—like he really meant it.

"I can come back another time," he offered, motioning down the hall. He was blushing, and it was adorable.

"No, no, it's okay. Really. Can you just give me a minute to throw on some clothes?"

"Sure," he said. He stood awkwardly in the doorway, not quite inside my apartment, but not quite in the hallway either.

"Is it okay if I come in?" he finally asked, and I waved him inside before running off down the hall to rummage through the clean but not yet folded basket of laundry that sat on my bedroom floor. I quickly slid my legs into a pair of sweatpants before pulling my arms through an off-the-shoulder crop-top, channeling a scene from *Flashdance* with my new ensemble. My dark hair was mussed in what I hoped was a sexy way, and as I glanced in the mirror before running out the door, I realized I had that 'just fucked' glow to my cheeks, courtesy of the porn I'd forgotten to turn off.

Perfect.

I padded down the hall and made my way back to the handsome stranger standing in my living room. His hands were in the pockets of his jeans, and he'd been unintentionally looking around my apartment, taking it all in. I could sense his nervousness; he was clearly uncomfortable, but his face lit up when he saw me coming, and for some reason, that was *the* moment for me. That was when I knew.

"You found some clothes!" Dylan cheered awkwardly.

"Would you like something to drink?" I asked, motioning toward the kitchen.

"Sure, some water would be great."

I pulled two bottles of water from the fridge and handed him one. "I'm sorry about before," I mumbled after a quick sip, although I was fairly certain he liked what he saw.

"Oh, it's no problem."

He cleared his throat and took a sip of water; I couldn't help but watch his Adam's apple bob up and down while he drank. Even *that* was sexy.

We took our seats at the table and sat in silence for an awkward beat, each of us drinking water like we'd die of thirst if we didn't take one more sip. I tucked a stray hair behind my ear before looking over at Dylan and opening my mouth to speak. But no words came out, they were stuck, so the silence continued, the air thick and riddled with sexual tension.

I'd never experienced such a loss for words.

"This is…" he said, trailing off. He cleared his throat again and visibly adjusted himself under the table.

"Are you okay?" I asked.

"I…yeah. I'm sorry, maybe I should go? I can come back another time." He stood, but didn't step toward the door, like he didn't actually want to go.

The next thing I knew, my lips were on his. I whimpered at the warmth of his mouth, and that was all it took for him to kiss me back—for his lips to travel along my cheek and down my neck, to my earlobes and then my clavicle. Every single nerve in me had been awakened.

But he pulled away, leaving me empty. I stepped back and brought a hand to my mouth to feel my swollen lips, the taste of him still lingering.

"I…I'm so sorry," he started. "I don't know what came over me. I…" I watched in a trance while he tried to make sense of the attraction between us. It was cute that he thought he had been the one to initiate the kiss. "I don't normally do this, I…wow, you're…"

I stepped forward and placed my hands on his chest, the

muscles taut beneath his shirt. He sucked in a breath, and I pressed my hips into him.

"There's absolutely no need to be sorry," I said, my voice low and sultry.

"No?" he asked, his mouth only millimeters from mine again. I outlined his bottom lip with my tongue, and he released an audible sigh before our mouths collided once more. He lifted me, his hands on my ass, and I wrapped my legs around him while we stumbled down the hall to my bedroom. He threw me onto the bed and reached for his belt buckle.

Again, he stopped abruptly, looking down at me, his face wary but his eyes filled with lust. "We shouldn't do this," he said. The bulge in his pants told me his appendage disagreed.

"Okay," I whispered. I pulled my sweater over my head anyway, watching his eyes grow wide as I slowly placed it around his neck and used it to pull him toward me. He studied me for a moment before he finally gave into temptation and removed his pants.

His lips met mine without further apprehension.

Beneath him, I wiggled out of my sweats and took in the sight of him. He was perfect, and I planned to claim every inch of him, maybe even more than once.

Hours later, I lay there in ecstasy while Dylan snored softly beside me. And I realized with a start that I was fucked, in the figurative sense. I'd broken every rule I had adhered to since the day Brandon had taken my virginity.

I had been greedy by not reciprocating oral.

I had screamed his name.

I even let him stay the night.

I was no longer winning at playing the game.

NOT THAT KINDA GUY

Dylan

THE WAY I SEE IT, it's no surprise that I'm dead. Not really, anyway. I mean, we all die at some point. We all have our time to go with the gods, or however the saying goes. That's not to say that I like the way I went out, though. Multiple stab wounds to the chest? Nope, didn't care for that.

The way I went out fucking sucked.

What I *am* saying is that my life ended with no regrets. I can't think of anything I would have changed, anything I would have done differently had the opportunity presented itself.

Alisha was it for me. She was my "meant to be"—my muse. The inspiration of my life. It's cheesy as hell, I know. I was once a skeptic, like you, so I get it.

I'm sure you don't see her the way I do, based on what you think you know about her. But come on, even Ted Bundy had a love of his life, and we all know how that turned out. I know I can't change the way you think about the woman I loved. What I can tell you is how I feel—how I *felt* —about her.

I wasn't sure what to expect the day I knocked on her apartment door. My grandmother was newly admitted into nursing care and had asked me to leave her house keys with Alisha, to explain to her that the house would be hers since she was no longer able to live on her own. I'd been working on the paperwork to gift the house to Alisha, not at all surprised that it would be going to her. I certainly had no desire to move out to the suburbs, so I was happy Grandma didn't ask me to take it.

But I knew about Alisha, who she was, and how Grandma had taken her in after her mother died.

Grandma loved that girl.

I knocked on her apartment door and couldn't have predicted the events that followed. She opened the door wearing nothing but a silk robe, and I could see her nipples poking through the thin fabric. Years later, I remember thinking back to that moment and still feeling a rush of blood straight to my dick. I immediately resisted the urge to pounce on her and instead chastely remembered I was a gentleman, cleared my throat, and looked off in the other direction.

Surprise number two: there was porn playing on the TV behind her, which I figured was the reason it took her so long to answer the door.

I barely heard anything she said after that, but I pointed to the TV, suddenly suffering from cotton mouth and unable to speak clearly. She ran to shut it off, hardly as embarrassed as one might expect her to be, considering the circumstances.

When her robe flew open, I about died.

This woman was insanely gorgeous, practically dripping with sexuality. There was an air of mystery to her, and I was immediately and completely enamored. For the life of me, I couldn't stop staring.

No wonder my grandmother kept me away from her until now.

The swell of her breasts beneath the thin robe quickly caught my attention again; it didn't matter that she had pulled it closed. I already knew what was under there. It was all I could do to look away when I wanted nothing more than to bury my face in her.

But I'm not that kind of guy, even if she was that kind of girl.

Not that it mattered. The next thing I knew I *was* buried inside her, and as crazy as it sounds, I knew she was about to change my life. We may have started things off with nothing more than raw sexual attraction, but she became so much more than that.

I couldn't get enough of her.

———

A woman with a tragic story was kind of my *thing*. I don't know why; I honestly couldn't have explained it if I tried. But I liked the way I felt with a woman like Alisha. There was something beautiful in the way she had herself convinced she didn't *need* me, even though her body seemed to think otherwise.

Eventually her mind did, too, much to her dismay.

Truth be told, I'd like to say things started off slowly with us, but you and I both know that would make me a liar, and that's one thing I refuse to be anymore. Alisha doesn't do anything slowly, and I really don't think I would have been able to handle it if she had. I was sold from the moment she opened that door.

The woman was sure to be the death of me.

And now that I think about it, I guess she was.

ALL FOR THE NOOKIE

Alisha

THEY SAY murder is a crime of passion, often premeditated. Deliberate. Now, I don't mean to say that *they* are fucking idiots...but *they* are definitely fucking idiots. Sometimes things just *happen*; they're not always premeditated and deliberate. Passion is meant for the bedroom.

I made this comment to my highly sought after attorney, Kyle Lanquist, and he told me to cut the shit. To shut up and stop talking unless I had something case-winning-worthy to share with him.

I didn't.

So, I shut my mouth. I let Kyle talk instead. Apparently, you're not allowed to disagree with statistics when you're on trial for murder.

Silly me.

I'm sure Kyle knows what he's doing. He seems to know his way around a courtroom, and he knows the law better than his own dick, so to a point, I guess I trust him. He *probably* knows his shit, statistically speaking.

But, if there's anyone who understands passion, it's me, and the idea of *passionately* murdering someone seems a little far-fetched. I think of *passion* in sexual terms only. As in, 'he seduced me with passion'. How can the same word be used to describe murder and death? I don't get it, and that's why *they* are fucking idiots. In fact, I passionately disagree with the statement.

See what I did there?

It's currently just after midnight and I'm lying on an uncomfortable mattress, alone in the dark within the confines of my cell. Lights out was a few hours ago, and I've tried desperately to sleep, I really have. But sleep isn't coming, and I doubt that it will tonight.

There's not much to do to pass the time after lights out, and I've already masturbated twice in hopes that my nerves will settle the hell down.

They haven't.

I'm not sure what else to do.

My body needs sleep.

I need to be rested for the first day of my trial tomorrow.

But all I can focus on is my visit with Kyle earlier today. For the hundredth time, we went over my trial strategy. We walked through my statement to the police, the order of events that occurred *that* day. And as usual, the visit dragged on for hours, with just the two of us crammed together in that stale room.

The air was so thick I could smell Kyle's breath when he spoke. He had onions with his lunch, most likely white as they're the most potent, and it seems he couldn't have been bothered to brush his teeth or at the very least chew a piece of gum before hot-boxing me in the interview room.

By the time Kyle finally quit flapping his jaws, I was so frustrated I nearly came on to him. Because, yes, that's how my mind works sometimes. Sex is a stress reliever for me so, despite the fact that hot onion breath radiated from his mouth for no less than three hours straight, I couldn't seem to get the idea of sucking Kyle's dick out of my head.

And let me make something clear: Kyle Lanquist is *not* a good looking man by anyone's standards.

But experience—and a long history of adults-only entertainment—proves that sometimes the least attractive of men carry around the greatest packages. How do you think some of these guys made such a career in porn? If I *had* made a move on Kyle, I simply would have adopted the no-kissing policy from *Pretty Woman*. Vivian knew what she was talking about when she penned that one.

I pondered the thought several more times by the end of our meeting, my desperate need for release nearly outweighing all of the obvious turn-offs. Plus, his dick was in close proximity on the other side of the table. It would be so easy to crawl under there and...

Who was I kidding? A CO was stationed outside the steel door, watching us from the 6x6 inch square window. There was probably even a camera.

Maybe he'd want to join in...

I needed to refocus, to clear my mind. Every time my thoughts drifted to something sexual, I did my best to refocus them somewhere else. I tried closing my eyes and just listening.

But Kyle's heavy breathing was all I could hear.

Then there was the blood. The pictures Kyle kept shoving

in my face, reminding me of the gruesome scene. Of my husband's mutilated body, the stab wounds, the knife in my hand.

I've never been a fan of blood.

And there was so much of it.

An awful, awful lot.

And the smell...don't get me started on the smell of it. The copper-like aroma lingered in my mouth, on my tongue, for days. I had nearly vomited at the sight of the photos. The pool of crimson soaking into the sheets, my husband's body sprawled haphazardly on our California king bed. The cast-off splatter on the once-gray walls, the streaks on the ceiling.

"Are you with me, Mrs. Thompson?" Kyle asked.

"Yes, I'm sorry," I muttered, shaking my head to clear the cobwebs.

"Good. It's important that we get through this today." He shuffled another set of papers in front of him. Police reports, evidence logs, and stacks of crime scene photos. There was so much to go through.

"Can you put those back in the folder?" I asked, pointing to the 8x10s strewn about the table. "They're making my stomach turn."

"Sure," Kyle agreed. "But as I've said multiple times, these photos will be shown in the courtroom throughout your trial. You really need to get comfortable around them." He stuffed the glossy photos into a manila folder and set it on the far edge of the table.

I crossed my arms over my chest, annoyed by his conde-scension. "That's pretty fucked up."

"What is?" he asked with a crooked brow.

"That I need to *get comfortable*, as you say, with photos of my dead husband."

Kyle let out an audible sigh. He was used to my outbursts,

my random mood swings. Not to say he was any less frustrated than the first time we met. His annoyance was written all over his face. He leaned over and rested his head on his hands, his elbows on the table as he looked over at me incredulously.

"Mrs. Thompson, you're on trial for your husband's murder."

"I realize that, Kyle, but that doesn't make looking at evidence of that fact any easier on me."

Kyle pointed a chubby finger at me and waved it around for dramatic effect. "Drop *that*," he said, waving his finger some more, "…attitude. We can't have that in the courtroom tomorrow."

I glared at him.

Kyle glared back.

We were at an impasse, my attorney and me. I realized right then and there that Kyle was not remotely convinced. My short, balding, thirty-something lawyer with onion breath was simply adhering to the parameters of his job description. His responsibility was to defend me, whether he thought I was innocent or not.

It was evident he did not.

Which meant that I was—yet again—fucked. But this time in the ass with no lube. Not even a thank you card.

I no longer wanted to suck Kyle's dick.

I pull the scratchy blanket up to my chin and try to remember the song my mother used to sing to me when I was a little girl and couldn't sleep. For the life of me, I can't recall the lyrics, but I still hear the melodic sounds of her voice. It soothes me, and I catch myself humming it quietly as I think of her; of her long dark hair, her deep amber eyes and sharp nose peppered with freckles. I can smell her perfume, the way the floral notes mixed with the menthol cigarettes she always smoked.

There was a time, I suppose, when she really did try to be a good mother.

It never lasted. As soon as I was old enough to do simple tasks on my own, Mom always went back to the bottle, she went back to using.

And I went off to kindergarten.

For years I wondered if she ever wished she could go back and do things differently. I never got the chance to ask her, and if I had, I'm not sure I would have. Something tells me I wouldn't have liked her answer.

But that afternoon was the start of it all—the calm before the chaos. After Brandon dropped me off at "home," I walked into Mrs. Maylen's house and let her goldendoodle, Teddy, outside for a quick pee in the backyard. Once he did his business, the two of us went back inside and hung out in the living room until Mrs. Maylen got home from work.

Her house was small and outdated—her husband, Frank, was long gone by then—but was much cleaner than our trailer and, truth be told, sitting in her house doing my homework with Teddy's head resting on my legs was always better than going home to my mom.

If she was even there.

So that's what I did for the next three hours.

Mrs. Maylen had told me on several occasions that I could help myself to the fridge and stay as long I liked, so I did. I think she had a good sense of what went on at my house and wanted to help in some small way. Not that I wanted to be a charity case, but Mrs. Maylen never once made me feel like one. So, I'd grabbed a can of pop from the fridge and made myself a turkey sandwich for dinner. It wasn't like my mother ever cooked for me anyway, and I would have been surprised if there was any edible food in the trailer.

Where things truly went wrong, and what I hadn't anticipated, was that my mother was across the street in our dilapidated, single-wide trailer, passed out on the dirty floor and wheezing through the last breaths she'd ever take. I chomped away on a delicious turkey, cheese, and mayonnaise sandwich while taking notes for my upcoming history test, and petting Teddy on his cute little fluffy head, completely unaware that the alcohol had finally taken my mother.

And because I'd done all of this with my Sony headphones glued to my head at max volume, while Fred Durst sang to me about how he did it all for the nookie, I didn't hear the sirens when the ambulance came and took my mother's lifeless body away. Her Fuck-of-the-Week had the wherewithal to call 9-1-1 when he realized she wasn't breathing, but lacked the basic human decency to stick around and wait for help to arrive.

Paramedics found her on the floor with her face in a puddle of vomit. She was pronounced dead on arrival. Darlene Hill was no longer my last living relative.

And because I didn't have a cell phone and hadn't told anyone where I was, after Mrs. Maylen came home from her nursing shift around nine p.m., I stuffed my homework into my backpack, walked across the street to our empty trailer, and climbed into bed.

The last coherent thought I had before falling asleep that night was *at least Mom isn't home to ruin my good day.*

THE TEN-DAY TRIAL

Alisha

I'LL NEVER MEET another man quite like Dylan Thompson. He was charming, in that I'm-kind-of-secretly-an-asshole way, but it worked for him. Because deep down, he wasn't an asshole at all. On the surface, he had a mama's boy look to him, but he was quick with the one-liners and one hell of a handyman around the house. He was caring and nurturing, but mostly, Dylan was a genuine soul. A beautiful mind, fused with a beautiful person.

He was also a god in the bedroom. We fucked every day —although Dylan preferred the term *made love*, but whatever. Truth is, I was impressed with Dylan's ability to keep up with me, to find ways to keep me just as satisfied physically as he did emotionally. No man before him had ever accomplished that—or even tried—not that there were many I let stick around for more than a couple times around the bases.

Dylan was rare in that regard.

I had become a quick fan of Tinder just before meeting Dylan. The dating app had simplified my hookup routine, and I had several dates on the calendar for that week. But Dylan asked me not to go, to cancel the dates, and shut down my profile entirely.

I laughed.

There was no way the man was serious. No way in hell.

Oh, but he was.

That probably makes him sound creepy, huh? Maybe a little...possessive? Yes, I can see how you might think that about him. But Dylan wasn't possessive at all. He wasn't creepy in the way you might think and didn't harbor any of the qualities of an ax-wielding murderer.

Maybe on paper, but not in the flesh.

It took me a little while to understand him. To see his love for what it was, and not what society and every horror movie plot deemed it to be.

Dylan was a simple man who proudly wore his heart on his sleeve. He trusted his gut, his intuition—which, let's be honest, got him killed in the end—and had no problem expressing his feelings. Somehow, he was even smart enough to know that the way to my heart wouldn't be an easy path, that it would require an intense amount of sex—trust me, it's not always a man's wet dream to hear that; it's a lot of pressure to burden them with—and the ability to put up with my mood swings.

But he was in it.

He wanted a chance to play his hand.

After canceling my Tinder date for the evening, I agreed to let Dylan hold me hostage in my own apartment for the next ten days.

"Give me ten days to win you over, and if you can honestly say you don't love me after ten days, I'll drag my ass through that door and never come back," he had said, pointing at the door. "I promise."

I agreed on one condition: that he put out at least twice a day, every day, throughout the ten-day trial period. You'd think I'd have thrown in something like, "and don't murder me with a chainsaw" or some shit like that, but apparently the only fear I had in that moment was that he wouldn't be able to keep up with my sex drive. He agreed without hesitation, and, just like that, I no longer required the services of my Tinder suiters.

I let them down as gently as I could, but the dick pics kept coming, filling my inbox with promises of pleasure and a generally good time. Any woman who's ever created a profile on a dating site knows what I'm talking about here. But Dylan and I managed to make a game of it, and some nights we would sit for hours looking closely at all the dick pics together, rating each of the packages. We even developed a scoring system—complete with color-coded charts—and printed the pictures out on heavy-duty card stock, taping them up on the wall above the couch. We ate delivery pizza while staring at fully erect penises and drinking black cherry pop until we declared one of them the Top Notch Dick.

Dylan even drew a crown on the winner's tip.

In retrospect, it helped that Dylan didn't seem to have a jealous bone in his body—a weight off my shoulders considering my profession, which he accepted with little concern. He liked that I didn't work more than a few nights a week, and my customers weren't the only ones that got off at the sight of my performance. Eventually Dylan even took to watching from across the room, off-camera but in perfect view from my perspective, sometimes with his dick in his hand.

I expected him to run by the fourth day.

But he stayed.

He kissed my forehead as I slept in his arms, and even helped with dishes after we cooked our first meal together.

By the eighth day, we seemed to have settled into a domesticated routine. It was confusing, but surprisingly comfortable, and I didn't know what to make of it. I couldn't believe I wasn't sick of him yet.

On the morning of the tenth day, Dylan worked from his laptop in my living room, preparing closing documents for a buyer while I watched my robot vacuum, Dustin Timberlake, clean the floors so I didn't have to. When he finally signed off and closed his laptop, he extended a hand to me and pulled me from the couch. Wrapping his arms around me, he kissed the tip of my nose and led me to the bathroom to join him for a shower.

We lathered and cleaned each other's bodies, and as soon as the last of the suds were washed away, he pushed me up against the wall and rubbed his growing erection against my backside. It had become a daily game for us, teasing each other until one of us couldn't take it anymore. And while I usually won our little torturous game, the thought that Dylan would probably be out of my life by the end of the day was enough to make me whimper in anticipation, my body begging to be taken by him.

I needed him.

He reached around, rubbing between my legs, quickly finding my clit and swirling a finger over the sensitive bud. With my tits pressed against the cold tile, I arched my back and he slid into me, claiming me from behind with slow, purposeful movements. I nearly cried out, but for the first time in my sexual history, I stifled my verbal approval.

I didn't want him to know how much my body needed him.

We moved together, instinctively building momentum, and suddenly nothing else mattered.

"Don't let this be the last time," he whispered in my ear, pumping harder and finding release quickly. He pulled out suddenly, groaning as I turned and dropped to my knees in front him, catching his load on my chest.

"My God, Alisha…" he mumbled through labored breath.

I licked the tip of his cock and stood to face him, kissing him deeply. "Let's move in together," he said with his lips still pressed to mine.

"Are you serious?" I asked, the shock surely written across my face.

"As a heart attack." He smiled deliciously, his mouth curving into a toothy grin, palm cupping my cheek. "I love you, Alisha. I have since the first day I met you, and I can't lose you."

"Yes," I blurted, the simple word taking me by surprise as it dropped from my mouth.

"Yes? As in…" He raised his brow.

"As in, yes, we should move in together," I confirmed. I searched his eyes for a tell that he wasn't serious, that he was merely acting on impulse and didn't actually want to live with me. But I saw nothing other than happiness in those eyes.

"And?" he coached.

"And, I love that we'll be able to do *this* every day," I said, wrapping my fingers around his length again. He pouted and his eyes crinkled; all I could do was look away.

Wrong answer.

"*Really?*" He huffed, pulling away and standing under the stream of water flowing from the shower head. I enfolded my arms around him and lured him back to me, not wanting to hurt him or let him believe for any reason that I didn't want this.

I can't lose you, either.

"I'm sorry, it's just that...*that*...is hard for me to say," I whispered.

"Then fucking nod or *something*," he snapped, frustration getting the best of him. "I need to know you love me back," he pleaded, his eyes searching mine. "This won't work if you don't feel the same. You know that, right?"

"I show you how I feel every day," I teased, running my hands down the muscles on his chest.

"This isn't about sex."

I sighed.

"Fine. I luh you," I mumbled, averting my eyes.

"You can do better than that..." he coaxed, his fingers trailing down my stomach. Softly and slowly, they worked their way inside me, his thumb flicking my clit, and I whimpered again, nearly buckling at the knees.

"Say it," he commanded. I steadied an arm against the slippery tile, my reserve dwindling with each flick of his thumb.

"I..."

He lowered his head, his tongue grazing my nipple as his thumb continued its reign of torture. "Love...yousofuckingmuch!" I cried out, my orgasm hitting me hard. Dylan's lips crashed down on mine, and it was everything.

Everything I never had.

Everything I never knew I wanted.

"That's my girl." He held me in his arms, under the water,

where I cried silently against his chest, grateful for the mask it provided for my tears.

Like the Grinch, my heart swelled to three times its size that day.

No one had ever told me they loved me.

WHERE'D YA GIT THEM JEANS?

Alisha

"ALISHA!" my mother's raspy voice yelled. I pushed my tenth-grade math books aside and climbed out of bed, turning down the hallway toward the living room. She was splayed across the torn couch, smoking a cigarette, the ash hanging off the end and about to fall onto her lap. Her dark hair was greasy, and the makeup from two nights earlier was still caked on her face.

"There's my girl," she slurred, a lazy smile stretching across her prematurely-wrinkled face. "Be a doll and grab your mother a beer, would ya?"

"Sure," I mumbled, crossing my arms and making my way to the kitchen, where a pungent odor loitered in the air. I glanced at the sink to find it stacked with plates caked in rotting food and several drinking glasses with curdled milk at the bottom.

I had stayed at Mrs. Maylen's just about every evening

after school that week, not returning home until after we shared a glass of milk and one of her famous oatmeal raisin cookies.

She never sent me home with an empty stomach.

Mom's crackhead friends had been in and out of the trailer, as if we had a revolving front door I didn't know about. I'd watched them come and go from across the street, knowing full well that whatever was going on inside was nothing I wanted to be a part of. Aside from the drugs, I wasn't naive enough to think my mother's male friends hadn't noticed me.

It was only a matter of time before one of them tried something. I did what I could to steer clear of them.

"Whatchya diddle daddlin' for?" Mom barked. I rolled my eyes, opened the fridge and snatched a generic beer from the otherwise bare shelf.

"Here," I said, handing the can to her. I pivoted as she grabbed my arm at the wrist, her bony hand cold against my skin.

"Where'd you git them jeans?"

I couldn't tell my mother that I had bought my jeans at Walmart with my own money. I'd outgrown most of my clothes in the last year, but I knew she would never waste her "hard earned" money on new clothes for me. She didn't even know that Mrs. Maylen was paying me to watch her dog, and if she had, she would've expected me to hand her the cash in exchange for room and board or some stupid shit like that.

As if it wasn't her job to provide food, clothing, and shelter for me.

"I borrowed them from Sara," I said nonchalantly, thinking on the spot with a shrug of my shoulders.

"Who's Sara?"

"Just a friend from school." I freed my arm from her

grasp and gestured toward the kitchen, making sure to offer up a half-cocked smile to appease her. "I'm going to do the dishes. Do you need anything else?"

Mom's bloodshot eyes shot back at me. She studied me again, focusing in on my jeans before cracking open the beer and taking a long sip. She settled the can on the rickety coffee table and let out a loud belch.

"Nope. Don't need nuthin' else," she slurred.

"Okay," I mumbled. I turned on my heel and went back to the sink, wishing I had a bandanna so I could cover my nose and mouth to rid my senses of the rotten odors that awaited me in that kitchen. Instead, I swallowed my wishful thinking and sighed, pulling my T-shirt over my nose and getting to work.

The next morning I took a freezing cold shower, thanks to a busted water heater that we couldn't afford to fix, and then tiptoed across the hall to my bedroom, careful to be extra quiet and not wake my mom. I was hoping to slip out for school without running into her at all.

I closed my bedroom door, locking it behind me and dropping my towel. Shivering, my arms and legs suddenly riddled with goosebumps, I quickly stepped into a fresh pair of underwear before pulling a sports bra over my head and stuffing my boobs into it as best as I could. Like everything else, the bra was too small, but it was clean. I made a mental note to bring a load of laundry with me to Mrs. Maylen's after school; she never minded when I used her machines, and it sure beat dragging a garbage bag full of clothes to the laundromat.

When my boobs were finally tucked away, I reached for

my new jeans, but instead of the familiar denim I expected, my fingers squished into something sticky.

The smell of fresh shit snaked into my nostrils.

I jumped to the other side of the room and flicked the light switch, holding my sticky hand out in front of me to inspect it. A brown goo was smeared between my fingers and underneath my freshly polished fingernails. I scooped my towel up from the floor and used it to wipe off my hand, realizing without a doubt that the substance in question was, in fact, human feces.

I peered down at the jeans at the end of my bed and noticed they were smeared with brown streaks, too.

My mother had taken a shit on my brand-new jeans.

SUDDENLY FEELING STUPID

Dylan

I GREW up in a decently-happy home—or homes, I should say, considering I split my time between two households—raised by divorced parents who after some-odd years apart, managed to co-parent decently together. I don't remember my parents ever fighting. Eventually, they both re-married. Dad and his wife moved out to Arizona, and I visited a couple times a year. Living with Mom full time was a bit much, I'll admit, considering that her new husband, Jim, brought along a son of his own—my stepbrother Sawyer. Once we got over the initial stepsibling bullshit, we were close for a bit, as teens and even as young adults.

Until we weren't.

Nonetheless, in retrospect, life was—dare I say it—fairly easy for me. I played on the varsity baseball team in high school, got good grades, and even had a long-term girlfriend —until I didn't. Other than getting my heart broken by a girl,

I never experienced anything close to the horrors Alisha faced growing up.

They say opposites attract, so I guess it made sense that we were made for one another. My only complaint was the fact that it took so long for us to find each other.

She completed me, just as I did her. Sorry for the *Jerry McGuire* reference there; I didn't even like that movie, but the line seemed fitting. I went off to college the fall after high school, and after graduating *summa cum laude* from the University of St. Thomas, I decided to stay in the Twin Cities.

Never once did I imagine I'd be living in a small suburban town like Buffalo, Minnesota. But that's where I ended up after meeting Alisha. I loved the hustle and bustle of Minneapolis, the skyline, the expansive floor-to-ceiling windows in my condo that overlooked the Mississippi River.

But Alisha hated it.

"Too many people," she'd said. She preferred the quiet of the smaller town, the privacy of our fenced-in backyard, the ability to see the stars clearly at night. Most of all, she loved the memories of my grandmother's house, and it was that admission that had me shoving my belongings into boxes and hiring a moving company less than two weeks into our relationship. Alisha closed on my grandmother's house, and I put the condo on the market.

And never once did I regret that decision.

When Alisha agreed to marry me I told her I'd move anywhere for her. Nothing else mattered, and with my job as a freelance Realtor I had the luxury of working anywhere. My condo sold quickly—well over the asking price—and I moved into my grandmother's house to be with my soulmate.

Admittedly, the house was several steps down in terms of luxury and modernization, but Alisha had plans to renovate, to bring the home up to standard with an expansive new kitchen and dining room, an open concept into the living room, and an en suite master bathroom fit for a B-List celebrity. She put her HGTV-inspired design skills to work and singlehandedly re-purposed a home filled with character.

We married only three weeks later, in a private ceremony at the nursing home, in front of my mother and stepfather—who weren't exactly in support of the marriage. I still wasn't speaking to my stepbrother, which my mother, of course, had thoughts about, but somehow managed to keep to herself. My grandmother was Alisha's maid of honor, alongside her friend, Chris, who I was growing fonder of each day. She had no one else, she had said. The thought was unnerving, but I intended to change that for her down the road.

She had only four contacts saved in her cell phone; me, my grandmother, Chris, and her hairdresser. She was adamant that no other numbers were worth saving, and the ones she didn't have could be found through a simple Google search.

Sometimes I envied my wife's simplicity.

But I accepted her as is; my new wife was a loner, happy on her own and nearly void of friends or family. The irony always intrigued me, but it was evident she did her best to keep people at bay, and I couldn't blame her.

"It's far better to be unhappy alone than unhappy with someone," she'd told me the night of our wedding, quoting the iconic Marilyn Monroe.

"What does that mean?" I asked, suddenly feeling stupid. It was such a simple saying, a generic concept really, yet I had a hard time comprehending it. What did I know? I was a popular jock in high school, and well liked in a decent-sized circle of friends, even as an adult. Although, if I'm being honest, that circle shrunk significantly during my years with Alisha. The nature of the beast, I suppose.

My new wife simply shrugged—as if the topic was fit for

nonchalance—and continued. "Other people make me feel lonely," she admitted sheepishly. "They're just *there*, taking up space, but not really present."

I nodded as if I understood, but I didn't, not really. All I knew was that I never wanted my wife to feel lonely again.

"Do you feel lonely right now?" I asked, pulling her close. She smiled and brought her lips to mine, stopping just before we touched, her minty breath warm on my face. She was good at that—at giving me just enough to keep me wanting more.

She had this devil-like grin that sucked me in every time; a spark in her eyes. "No," she said, smiling. And our mouths molded together, our lives officially intertwined, my wife and me.

Perhaps it was destiny, who knows?

Nonetheless, little by little I learned more about her past. About her childhood and the incompetent mother who raised her. About the father she never knew, the man she had never met. Grandma hadn't mentioned how bad things were for her before she'd taken her in, but I knew enough to know enough.

And all of that, everything I learned over time, only made me love her more.

She had my heart—all of it.

Until the very end.

DECEIT'S FAVORITE ROLE

Alisha

FRIENDS ARE a rare commodity in my world. I've never had many, aside from Dylan and Mrs. Maylen. And Chris, but we'll get to him later. Everyone at school hated me—unless they were involved with me sexually, of course, and even then they often ended up hating me in the end—and I found that being alone was simply easier. There was no one to let me down, no one to judge me or drone on about the dramas of their life. No one to lie, cheat, beg, borrow, or steal.

When you grow up with a mother like mine, the silence can be comforting. I guess that kind of stuck with me.

Kyle suspects my lack of friends will be an issue of concern during the trial; there really isn't anyone left to speak on behalf of my character—not positively, anyway. Personally, I think that's bullshit, but my opinion rarely seems to matter. How is it my fault that women have always hated me?

And men? Well, they only hate me when their wives are around.

So, naturally, when the story of my husband's murder hit the local news I was the first and only suspect the media honed in on, thanks in part to my perpetual loner status, coupled with the fact that the spouse is *almost* always to blame.

Plus, my alibi was horse shit.

Channel 5 News pounced first. Their overly made-up, camera-ready reporter was outside on my lawn with her news crew before I was even arrested. It didn't matter that they had yet to establish a narrative—they heard murder and came running. Public speculation was sure to do the rest of the work for them.

Let the pieces fall where they may.

Alisha Thompson, the wife of Dylan Thompson, a Buffalo, Minnesota man who was found stabbed to death in their home this morning, looks to be the prime suspect in his brutal murder.

Of course, I *was* alone during the window of opportunity, off on my morning run along Griffing Park Road. Other than a nosy neighbor who happened to peer out her kitchen window as she guzzled her morning coffee in her slippers and fuzzy bathrobe, there wasn't a single person to corroborate my story. It didn't help that I headed out for my run nearly two hours earlier than usual since I was having trouble sleeping, on account of the argument we'd had the night before.

Police say neighbors of the couple reported that thirty-year-old Alisha Thompson was seen leaving the home during the very early hours of the morning, just before five o'clock. She was described as "distraught" and one witness suggested she appeared to be "on a mission".

The house was suffocating me.

Every corner of every room was a reminder of what I'd lost. I needed to get out, to inhale fresh air into my lungs, to feel the ground at my feet. I climbed out of bed, slipped into my yoga pants and sports bra and slid my feet into my running shoes. Downstairs I stopped in the kitchen for a bottle of water, and scribbled a note to my husband—who I'd abandoned in the bed that I'd just crawled out of.

The note was just in case.

Admittedly, my choice of words, what I wrote on the back of that grocery receipt, weren't ideal. I suppose I could have written something more likely to have come from a loving wife.

It wouldn't have killed you to tell the truth.

Those are the words I chose to leave behind. The message I felt necessary to jot down on a wrinkled receipt before taking off for a run to clear my head.

I was angry.

Dylan was angry.

Our fight had been monstrous.

The note—found in our trash bin—was confiscated by investigators for evidence, and would be used against me in a court of law.

My iPhone was left behind to charge on the kitchen counter.

There was no record of my whereabouts that morning, even though the GPS tracking app Dylan had installed on it would have otherwise provided law enforcement with significantly useful information.

By my estimation, I was out of the house no longer than thirty minutes.

Thompson, former host of the popular adult streaming website LishasBedroom.com, has no other social media presence, and sources from Mr. Thompson's immediate family say she has been a quote, "thorn in their side", since the day she and Mr. Thompson met. They say she has no friends, that she takes pleasure in embarrassing them with her profession, and that Mr. Thompson was completely infatuated with her.

The general population had a hard time accepting the fact that any sane person would choose to work in my profession, a career entirely based on looks, sexual fantasies, and what they consider "deviant" behavior. I mean, why focus elsewhere when the sex-obsessed, friendless wife of the victim fits the mold *so* well?

Viewers ate that shit up—the media's notion of a jealous lover, a lonely wife. Vindication. It sure made for good TV. Hell, even I would have watched it.

To make matters worse, the most damning piece of evidence in the prosecution's arsenal is the fact that I was standing right there, in the middle of the crime scene, wielding what would later be confirmed to be the murder weapon, when the police busted through the door.

A chef's knife taken from the woodblock in the very kitchen I stood in earlier that morning.

With a gun pointed at my chest, an officer coerced the knife from my trembling hands as blood dripped from it onto the carpet.

I stood, frozen in place, unable to move or speak, staring down at my husband's mutilated body, at the seventeen stab wounds, still fresh, in his chest.

Because of me.

Neighbors also reported hearing screams coming from the Thompson family home that morning. They heard yelling in the late hours of the night, a common occurrence from the Thompson household, they said.

What the media failed to understand, and subsequently gave zero fucks about, is that sometimes people scream when they're frustrated. They fight and argue when they're scared and in need of someone to blame, because that's the only way they get through it. Sometimes it's the only immediate relief for those endorphins so they don't suffocate from within.

So, yes, I screamed.

Because I was angry.

My husband had just confessed a devastating secret.

Mrs. Thompson has declined to comment. We'll have more on this developing story. For now, I'm Lexy Dawson, reporting for Channel 5 News.

———

I like to eat my meals alone these days, as with any other activity in lockup. Sometimes the other women like to fuck with me—they'll cat call or grope me when I walk by. But most days they leave me alone since I don't play into their childish games.

As difficult as it is to refrain, I'm trying here.

Kyle says a clean record in lockup could lead to lesser sentencing. Today, however, it seems I've made an accidental friend, a confidant, if there is such a thing in prison.

"So, did ya do it?" Tiffany asks. She winks and offers a coy smile as she shoves a plastic fork full of tasteless scrambled eggs down her gullet. She's beautiful, like me, only in a completely different way. Her blonde hair is chopped to her shoulders, her eyes an amber tone I haven't seen on many women. When she lifts her fork I notice the scars on her forearms, alongside a shitty tattoo of the word, *overcome*.

"No," I say, meeting her eyes.

"That's what they all say." She laughs. It's soft, almost pretty, but also mocking in a way. It pisses me off.

"Did *you* do it?" I snap.

"Yep."

I stop chewing and watch her face. She's stoic and doesn't blink as she dares me to challenge her further. I'm not at all familiar with her case, but I believe her, based on the creepy ass look in her eyes. I don't doubt for a second that Tiffany is capable of murder.

I also don't doubt that this woman is proud of whatever she's done. And I can't help myself, I want to know what she did. I *need* to know.

"Why?" I ask, and she shrugs like all I've asked her is what she wants for dinner.

"He deserved it."

I don't say anything, just spoon another bite into my mouth and wait for her to continue. It's silent as we chew, each waiting for the other to speak.

She caves first.

"Bastard liked to put his hands on me," she says. Her tone hushed, like she enjoys the mystery of it, and doesn't want anyone else to hear her confession.

"That seems to be a common theme in here."

"It's a common theme everywhere, gorgeous." She tucks a strand of stringy hair behind her ear, and I notice another small scar just above her earlobe. "Most of us are just too fucking chicken shit to do anything about it."

"If he was abusive, then what are you doing in here? Wouldn't killing him fall under self defense?"

"Sure," she shrugs. "*If* he had been the aggressor the night I killed him." She wants me to ask, and I swear I'm not going to, but I have to know, so I do.

"I'm not following." I sit back in my chair and cross my arms over my chest.

She sighs and rolls her eyes, as if she's annoyed I haven't figured it out yet. She's not.

"It was premeditated," she says. "I planned it. Thought about it for months, really." I don't engage further, just continue watching her.

Her shoulders slump, and she leans over the table, her breasts dipping into her plate of eggs. "I couldn't take the abuse anymore and knew he'd never give me a divorce. He'd never let me leave him. So, I went out and bought a gun, and then I waited for him to come home from work. Shot him when he pulled into the garage, and then went back to boiling noodles for my manicotti. I knew it'd be my last supper." She pauses for effect and then shakes her head in disbelief, staring down at her plate and pushing the food around like it had done something to piss her off. "It's a shame; I was a damn good cook."

We sit in silence again, each of us eyeballing the other. I'm not sure if she's playing me, but in that moment I choose to believe her.

"Was it worth it?" I ask.

"Yep." She picks up her tray and stands before leaning down and speaking into my ear. "A friendly word of advice? Stop claiming your innocence in here. Whether you did it or not doesn't matter. You're already here, mixed in with a group of murderers and sociopaths. Saying you *didn't* do it only makes you look weak. It puts a target on your back. So either start lying or go fucking kill someone and earn your stripes."

She straightens and turns on her heel, and I watch her walk away. I smile as she looks over her shoulder and winks, the realization that she's just fed me a delicious line of bull-shit sinks in.

"Deceit's favorite role is that of the victim," I say to no one but myself.

SIMPLY HER

Dylan

I WASN'T PERFECT, okay?

Everyone kind of has their *thing*. Their guilty pleasure, the one secret they keep from everyone else, be it from embarrassment, shame, or otherwise. I was big on not keeping secrets from Alisha. I wanted her to be honest with me—even if the truth was difficult to hear—and in return, I vowed to do the same for her.

Only I didn't.

I'd been lying to her since the day I met her. Because once I met her, little to nothing else mattered more than keeping her. I no longer cared about money—although, between the two of us, we had plenty of it—or my family, my friends. Not even my career—not that it suffered, really. I just worked less.

I had my woman, the one with whom I'd spend the rest of my life, and I cared less and less about everything else. That's probably where I went wrong.

That's probably where things began to fall apart for me.

I stopped questioning things. I stopped sleeping with my eyes open, and instead, with her in my arms, reveled in the smell of her shampoo and the sensation of running my fingers up and down her toned arms. The soft skin that lined them was a newfound addiction for me.

I missed all the signs.

Every damn one of them.

Because the only thing in my line of sight was her. Did I regret it in the end? Did I beg to go back and do it all over again, to do it all differently?

Nope.

Not even for a second.

I didn't even regret the lies.

But despite Alisha's profession, despite her utter beauty and near-genius mind, my lovely wife lacked confidence. She truly had no idea how amazing she was; she didn't know her worth. I guess that's what a childhood full of bullshit and let-downs will do to a person. I worked tirelessly to prove that she was more than deserving of love. To prove she was worthy of every single thing this world had to offer.

I wooed her, even though I didn't have to.

I took her out on dates, showed her around Minneapolis, introduced her to new and expensive cuisines, because even after she grew her wealth, she still ate TV dinners and takeout and frozen lasagnas. She hated to cook. I bought her nice clothes, even though she didn't need them and clearly could have afforded them herself. I took her to get her hair done, her nails. She loved it. She had never been pampered before, and it wasn't like anyone had ever taught her these things— she didn't know what she had been missing.

And I loved being the one to show her that side of life, the joy of being taken care of. I'm sure you think I'm crazy, that I'd lost my damn mind, right? Meh. That's fine. Really. It's not like it changes anything. But I get it, I do.

Who would give up everything for a woman like that?

Me, that's who.

If you'd met her, you'd understand. She was a majestic creature you couldn't look away from him. A goddess. But my infatuation with Alisha stemmed from so much more than sex, I promise. I'm sure you think that's a complete line of bullshit—it's really not. *I* had a hard time keeping up with *her*, so trust me, it wasn't the sex that had me wrapped around her finger. It wasn't even her strikingly beautiful face and her better-than-super-model body, either.

It was simply *her.*

And let me tell ya, if you don't know what I mean then you better question whether or not you really love your significant other. Truly. Because if you did, you'd understand exactly what I'm talking about.

You'd get it.

You'd have told the lie, too.

You won't learn all that much about me when all is said and done, because I assure you, I existed for the sole purpose of loving Alisha Thompson.

And that's what I did—until the day I died.

PSYCHO-BABBLE BULLSHIT

Alisha

MY MOTHER HAD a way with words. She was the best at spewing them, even when they made no sense in the order she chose to spit them out. She was, after all, always drunk or high or both, and only present when she wanted to be—or when her unemployment funds dried up and she couldn't even afford a pack of smokes. So, when I say my mother had a way with words, it wasn't that she was *good* with them; she simply used a lot of them.

They made good weapons.

Her favorite thing to do was degrade me, to rant about how ugly I was, how incompetent and useless I had become. As a kid, and even as an adult, these words haunted me. But at that age, as a teen, I didn't know if they were true or not; I hadn't yet tested their validity in the real world. Instead, I learned to take each spiteful word with a grain of salt and eventually realized her love of putting me down stemmed from nothing less than jealousy.

She wanted what I had.

What substance abuse had taken from her.

"I swear, you're the ugliest girl on the planet, Alisha," she once said, waving her arm around as if to demonstrate the entire planet she was referring to. I hadn't said a word to initiate the conversation; she simply blurted it out during a commercial break. *Roseanne* was no longer entertaining her, so it was time to harass me instead. I looked up from the book I was reading and debated whether or not to engage. Sometimes saying nothing is the best response to criticism.

She chugged from her beer, emptying the can and tossing it across the living room.

"Whatcha readin' for, anyway? S'not gonna make ya any prettier." She laughed at my expense, pleased with herself as if what she'd said were actually funny.

"It's for English class," I said, paying her little attention.

"Don'tcha know men prefer skinny girls? None a them'r gonna want a curvy girl like you."

"Okay." I went back to reading and considered leaving the room. I knew it wouldn't help, though. It would only instigate the situation further. She'd follow me and then lash out for disrespecting her and walking away while she was talking to me. As if respect was a word in her vocabulary.

Best to wait for the show to come back on. Then she'll forget about me.

"Git me another beer, will ya?" she asked. I marked the page in my book and got up from the frayed recliner, making my way to the kitchen. The fridge was empty, save for a half-eaten box of pizza, the beer gone.

"You're all out."

"Don't fuck with me child," she barked, sticking another

cancer stick in her mouth and lighting the tip with a match. She inhaled and then withdrew the cigarette from her lips, holding it between her fingers, the smoke like fog floating around her lips as she spoke. "Well, don't jus' stand there. Go out and git some more."

"I don't have any money."

"Fuck, child, neither do I. Find some. Go sell that ridiculously curvy body of yours on the street corner or sumthin'. See if it's worth anything."

I was fourteen years old and stared at my mother blankly, trying to convince myself that she hadn't just encouraged me to sell my underage body on the street corner.

But she had.

And not for the first time.

I didn't know what to do. I wasn't old enough to buy beer even if I had the cash, but getting out of there for the night was the only thing on my mind. So, I grabbed my coat and book bag and went across the street to Mrs. Maylen's house, where I stayed for the next six days.

My mother never once checked in on me.

———

Mrs. Maylen took me in after my mother's overdose.

Sometimes I have a hard time understanding why she did it, but most days I'm nothing but grateful. Her own daughter had been out of the house for years, already with a family of her own and a couple kids. She said she could use the company. I had no other living relatives that I knew of—I've never met my father, and my mother always claimed she didn't know his last name so he wasn't even listed on my birth certificate. CPS didn't take issue when Mrs. Maylen offered to foster me, and I was able to move in with her right away.

It was confusing at first, having someone who cared about me. The first weekend I stayed with her, she took off a couple shifts at the hospital and helped me clean out Mom's trailer—most of which we donated or tossed in the shared dumpster—and together we packed up my bedroom. I moved across the street with little more than three small boxes. She said she didn't want me to become another orphan lost in the system just because no one wanted to foster a seventeen-year-old girl.

If I were a Southerner, this is where I'd insert the sympathetic, "bless her heart."

That also meant she expected me to go to college. I did well in school and ended up earning a full ride to St. Cloud State, which is the only reason I was able to attend college at all. My mother had left nothing behind. No life insurance, no savings. Just a rundown trailer full of ratty furniture and overflowing ashtrays.

It still amazes me how a proper parental figure can change the entire course of a person's life. For the first time ever, I had a curfew. Dinner was on the table every single night, and most nights I even helped cook. I had to ask permission to make plans, and Mrs. Maylen had to approve of them. A typical teenager and newly orphaned child likely would have rebelled at such structure, but I reveled in it.

Somebody finally cared about me enough to worry. Enough to put rules in place that kept my ass parked on the couch doing my homework instead of out on the streets experimenting with the very drugs that made me an orphan in the first place.

I didn't cry when I learned that my mother was dead. The tears never came; I didn't need them.

I wasn't sad.

I hadn't loved my mother since the day she sent me off to kindergarten and didn't pick me up because she was passed out on our living room couch. I knew, even then, that love is a two-way street, and she was driving down a one-way road.

My teacher, Mrs. Ronzon, had given me a ride home when five o'clock ticked by and she still hadn't shown. I'll never forget the look on her face when we pulled up to the trailer.

"Would you like me to walk you to the door? Do you have a key?" she asked, tentatively shifting the car into park.

"No, thank you," I said quietly, shaking my head. "We don't lock the door."

"I'll wait here to make sure you get inside, okay?"

I nodded and removed my seatbelt. "Thanks, Mrs. R."

I got out of the car and jogged excitedly to the front door, as if I were thrilled to finally be home. Mrs. R didn't need to know that I wasn't. A foul smell instantly smacked me in the face, and I spotted my mother passed out on the couch. She was sprawled on her stomach, her left arm hanging heavily over the edge and a spent cigarette in the ashtray, burned down to the filter.

I pasted a smile on my face and turned back to Mrs. R, giving her a thumbs up. I could see her sigh with relief when she placed her hand over her heart and waved goodbye before backing out of the driveway.

These days, a situation like that would've sent me straight to foster care.

Kristin and I spoke about my mother often. She was adamant my mom was the source of my detachment issues—and in hindsight, sure, she probably was. Any idiot could make that assumption. But it was Kristin's roundabout way of getting there that irked me.

"Do you feel emotion, Alisha?" she asked, her chin tilted. We were forty minutes into our session, focused only on the topic of my mother, and she'd just finished a spiel on nature versus nurture, of which I wasn't entirely sure which side of the proverbial fence we'd landed on.

"What kind of question is that?"

"Humor me. Do you *feel?*"

"Of course."

"Show me." She waved her hand, as if doing so offered some insight as to what the hell she wanted me to say.

"What do you mean?"

"Show me happy," she said, nonchalant, as if I were an actress auditioning for a play. I suppose I was a performer of sorts, considering my profession. Yet, I stared at her blankly, as I often did, and tried to anticipate where the line of questioning was going. "What makes you happy?"

"I don't know."

"There has to be something"

"Sex."

"Okay, how about sadness? Do you ever cry?"

"No."

"Do you get sad?"

"Not really."

"How do you feel right now?"

"Annoyed."

"That's fair. Do you feel angry?"

"Not really."

"Hmm…" She started writing on her legal pad. The room was silent for a few minutes while she scribbled her psycho-babble bullshit onto the page. "When was the last time you remember feeling angry?"

My face contorted, and I pretended to ponder the question. Anger wasn't necessarily my thing, despite my upbringing. I'm fairly certain one has to feel some sort of connection to something, or someone, in order to feel anger, and for the most part, I cared little about anything.

That cord had been disconnected a long time ago.

"When my mother forgot to pick me up from school on the first day of kindergarten."

"That was the *last* time you felt angry about something?"

"Probably," I said, shrugging my shoulders.

She looked at me in disbelief and then returned to her notes, her head lowered for several minutes. I cleared my throat after five minutes passed without a word. The silence was becoming awkward.

"I think that'll be it for today," she said, looking up at me and removing her reading glasses.

"We still have fifteen minutes…" I reminded her. Not that I wanted to stay, but she'd never once ended a session early, and I didn't know what to make of it.

"You did well today, Alisha." She stood and placed her notebook and pen on the desk, motioning to the door.

I left that day never understanding what made her end the session so abruptly. The following week I was preoccupied with my husband's murder.

I haven't seen Kristin since.

FESTERING BENEATH THE SURFACE

Alisha

I TALK TO HIM.

Dylan.

Sometimes it's like he's right beside me, like he's here with me. I feel the warmth of his lips against my skin, his fingers trailing my body. I don't know how or why it happens, but I cherish these premonitions, these unexpected visits from him.

I long to hear his voice, to undo what I've done. I would write to him in a journal if I didn't think it'd be used against me as evidence. I don't trust that it won't fall into the wrong hands. So, the one-sided conversation resides in my head, never to be repeated. Never to be misconstrued for something it's not.

I miss you, and I don't know what to do with that. You come to me in my dreams at night, and you're as beautiful as ever. I hold you, because I know one of these times it will be for the last time. Why did you have to break us?

I'd give anything to breathe you in, to inhale the scents of you—your skin, your hair, your breath. I'd taste your lips, your cock. My body needs you in ways I can't explain.

It's not fair, what I've done to you. What you've done to us. But life never is, is it, baby?

Ironically, it was my mother who taught me that, and I'm ashamed to admit I caught myself missing her the other day, too. I wasn't sure what to make of it. But I craved her honesty for reasons I can't explain. I needed her raw sense of truth.

She came to me in a dream, too—much like Dylan often does. She was the version of herself that didn't suck, before all the drugs. Before the drinking and uninvited house guests. I was a little girl, only four, and she sang to me as I drifted to sleep, running her fingers through my hair, my head in her lap. She was sober, and still beautiful in the intoxicating way she once was. Some would say I look like her in pictures. How she looked before she was no longer beautiful.

"Don't get too used to this," she says quietly.

"Why not?" I ask, looking up at her, my voice tiny and full of wonder.

"It never lasts, sweetheart."

I lay my head back on her lap, a sigh escaping my lips.

Mother always knew best, even when she didn't.

"Thompson, you have a visitor," CO Marin barks, stepping into my unlocked cell. Kyle didn't mention coming by today, so her announcement startles me.

"Who?"

"Dunno," she says. "Get dressed, let's go."

I pause for a moment, the idea of an unexpected visitor leaving a sour taste in my mouth. "If it's not my lawyer, I'm not interested."

CO Marin gives me a hard look, visibly debating whether to force me down to the visitor's parlor, and I stare back, unintimidated by her posturing. She sighs and stomps off, and I almost feel bad at the thought that my visitor—whoever they are—has inconvenienced her or any of the other staff here. They would have had to run them through the security screening, and I hear they're pretty swamped down there. I'm not out to piss anybody off, but I didn't ask for a visitor, either.

Not that any of the women get them often; most of their families, their men, abandon them once they end up in here.

But if it wasn't Kyle, who else would visit me here?

Officer Marshall's hand wraps around my throat before I have a chance to realize he's in the hall. I'm usually more alert, more aware of his presence. Without warning, he shoves me against the wall, and the other women scatter, like roaches in the spotlight.

CO Jones is gone, too.

He grabs my face with a rough hand and shoves his pelvis into mine, anchoring me against the wall as I turn away, my face pressed against the cold brick. "I've been watching you for years," he taunts, his tongue rough like a cat's along the length of my cheek. "And how lucky for me that you're *here* now."

My eyes bore into his, daring him to touch me again, except I don't actually want him to touch me. Everyone seems to think because of my profession that I'm free game. People here know who I am, and they've made the assumption that I'm guaranteed to lie back and spread my legs to them, inviting them in on an assembly line. What they're quickly learning is that I'd rather fuck myself with my own hand than let any of them touch me.

Officer Marshall doesn't like that. He doesn't care for my lack of interest in his pleasure toy. But there is no doubt there, in his eyes, as he stares me down. He knows nobody will stop him from getting what he wants.

They never do.

"No one will ever believe a slut like you," he declares through gritted teeth. His nostrils flare and he lets out a guttural moan, his hands tearing at my clothes, untucking my shirt, his fingernails scratching the surface of my skin. "Don't act like you don't fucking want it, Thompson. I *know* you do."

I kick at his ankles and make an attempt to scream, but his hand covers my mouth before anything audible comes out. He pants like a dog, moaning as he manages to slide my pants down my waist, further stifling my ability to kick free. He hovers there, the weight of him immobilizing my arms and pinning me to the wall. Perspiration drips from his forehead, and I try to breathe.

To mentally go somewhere else.

I loosen my muscles and succumb to his power, realizing I won't be able to stop what he's about to do. He *will* have his way with my body.

But he will not have *me*.

There's relief in his eyes when he feels my body relax, and I close my eyes and tell myself he's Dylan, that I want this. I don't want to remember Officer Marshall's face when this moment haunts me later.

"Good girl. I knew you wanted this," he says. "Fuck," he mutters, pinning me down with one arm. He flips me over and enters me from behind, wasting no time building momentum.

I'm wet, even though I don't want this.

The anger bubbles inside of me as he fucks like a wild animal in season. I try to bring myself somewhere else, but all I see is red...I see blood. *So much blood. And it pools beneath his body and drips from my hands, outwardly flowing because of me. Because of these urges I can't control, can't stop.*

Officer Marshall groans, snapping me from my reverie. My eyes pop open instinctively, though I don't want them to, and he pulls out, shaking his load onto my ass. I turn my head, still pressed against the wall, and it's Shelly Farber who stands watch at the end of the corridor this time. She's peeking—the naughty girl—watching me get fucked like she's jealous it isn't her.

She hasn't had her turn yet.

He knows how much she wants it.

I feel unclean, suddenly in need of a shower but knowing I won't get one until morning. He stuffs his dick into his boxers and zips his pants, tapping my backside to let me know it's okay to come off the wall, but he places a possessive hand on my hip and leans in, whispering in my ear.

"You've always been my favorite, Lisha."

His eyes are dark, still dilated from the high of the chase, the penetration he didn't deserve. I say nothing, although I'd like nothing more than to spit in his face. His semen still covers my ass and he hands me a wad of paper towels that he pulls from his back pocket as casually as a dog owner picking up shit with a plastic bag. I take them and he thinks I will thank him, like the others, but I'm not grateful.

I don't thank him.

He turns and makes his way down the corridor toward Shelly Farber.

He whistles as he walks.

"Let's go, playmate. Back to lockup," he calls out in a singsong tone.

I use the wad of paper towels to wipe him off me before pulling up my pants. One foot in front of the other, I follow Officer Marshall, guilt building with each step as I chastise myself for coming right along with him.

I feel that anger now, that missing emotion Kristin once spoke of. It's here, festering beneath the surface like acid.

And I fucking hate it.

UNEMPLOYMENT-VILLE

Alisha

I STILL HAVEN'T TOLD you how I ended up working in the sex industry. It's not that I'm ashamed of what I do—what I did. My work was perfectly legal and safer than stripping at a club. Is it something I ever admitted to Mrs. Maylen? No. But that'd be like confessing your darkest sins to your grand-mother, and who the hell would do a thing like that? The woman would have had an aneurysm if she knew what I did to earn a living.

So I didn't tell her.

And neither did Dylan, because I'd sworn him to secrecy. I honestly don't think he would have been able to tell her even if he wanted to, though. It was hard enough when his parents found out. It was a whole thing, and awkward as all hell when we discovered that his own father was a paying subscriber.

Imagine *his* surprise when Dylan texted him a photo of us

together. Dylan was so proud of his new girlfriend, and certain my profession wouldn't be an issue because no one would ever find out about it.

But they did.

Even the purest humans often can't resist temptation. And what better way to indulge in one's sexual fantasies than via the internet in the privacy of your own home?

It's no secret that sex sells. I tried to go a different route, truly I did—it just didn't work out for me. I started my first full-time job right out of college. I was twenty-two and had otherwise earned my spending money as a part-time barista, but the paycheck was no longer cutting it—I'd recently rented an apartment and had no choice but to get a decent job to pay the rent. And while an office job was sure to bore the living shit out of me, I was prepared to do it, to stake my claim in the workforce as a Monday through Friday nine-to-fiver.

It took an embarrassingly short amount of time for me to realize how unfit I was for corporate America, and my first day on the job also happened to be my last.

Drew Milner, the lucky fuck who had the pleasure of employing me, greeted me at the reception desk on the ground floor of a sky-rise building in downtown Minneapolis. My new boss, due to a scheduling mishap, wasn't the person I initially interviewed with the week earlier, so our first encounter occurred right then and there. He was visibly displeased from the moment he took a look at me as he rounded the corner coming off the elevator.

Why? I hadn't a clue, but I was determined to put my best foot forward with this job, to turn a lasting impression into a regular paycheck.

But my arms were full, and evidently the impression I'd given wasn't one he was interested in. In one hand I carried a small box of personal belongings to decorate my new desk—

for no reason other than that cliches told me that's what you're supposed to do when you work in an office. In the other, a travel mug filled with coffee, and my most successful garage sale find to date—a knock-off designer purse I was quite proud of despite my disdain for expensive things. Sometimes I just wanted to fit in, what can I say? But because of this, because I cared more about filling my arms with "stuff", I couldn't shake Drew's hand. Instead we more or less nodded in each other's direction.

"Alisha Hill?" he asked with a raised brow.

"Yes! Drew? Hi, it's so nice to meet you."

"Likewise. I see you've got your hands full there. Need some help?" He reached for my box of trinkets, and as he did, his hand brushed against my breast. I hoped it was an accident, but his face seemed to say otherwise—he wasn't phased by it and didn't acknowledge the mishap, so I didn't either.

I adjusted my shirt with my now-free hand and followed him down the hall, my nerves rattled. "Thank you," I said, doing my best to ignore the incident the same way he had.

The elevator ride was awkward at best, the seconds ticking by as if in slow motion. We barely spoke, and the few times I wanted to say something, I found myself biting my tongue instead.

Once off the elevator, we reached a pod of cubicles, and Drew gestured to the empty desk that would be mine, motioning for me to step in first.

Or so I thought.

I realized my mistake when we bumped into each other, and this time he walked directly into my backside, and managed to grab my ass in the process.

"I'm so sorry—" I started, the apology rolling off my tongue as I turned to face him. He set the box on my desk and held up his hand, speaking in a hushed tone more suited for a library.

"It's fine. Listen, maybe you should run home and change? I can push your first training session out to ten o'clock."

I ran my hands over my clothes, certain I must have spilled coffee on my outfit.

"Excuse me?"

He raked a hand through his hair before shrugging and motioning to me again. "You can't dress like that here," he said. The trajectory of his eyes contradicted his words. It was evident he liked what he saw.

"Like *what*?" I asked, challenging him to grow a pair and explain himself.

"Like...*that*." He gestured at me incredulously, making an effort not to look me in the eye. "It's...*provocative*."

"Nothing I'm wearing goes against the office dress code," I argued, certain the rebuttal was accurate. "I checked." More than once actually, just to be sure I was dressed appropriately for my new job. Mrs. Maylen always told me to *dress for the job you want, not the job you have*, so I was channeling my inner Gretta by donning a pencil skirt that fell below the knee and three-quarter-sleeved white blouse buttoned high enough to hide my cleavage.

Is it the heels? Are they too high? The wrong color? Should I have worn nylons?

"Well, I happen to disagree and would be more comfortable if you'd head home and cover up. This is a place of business."

His assessment didn't sit well with me, and immediately I knew I didn't belong in an environment like that. "*You* would be more comfortable? Are you fucking kidding me?" I snapped, unconcerned with the rising volume of my voice.

I fought the urge to slap him, if only on account of the many witnesses whose heads were starting to pop up like whack-a-moles over the tops of the cubicles. Instead, I turned and grabbed my box from the desk before stomping back toward the elevator.

"So we'll see you back here at ten then?" he semi-shouted, trying not to further disturb the staff.

"Nope," I said, not looking back.

I hadn't expected to be sexually harassed on my first day of work, no less than fifteen minutes after entering the building. With my never-to-be-unpacked box of supplies tucked under my arm, my coffee abandoned on the desk, and my pride dangling by a thread, I was in the elevator on a ride straight back down to Unemployment-ville, population seven million, give or take.

To top it off, rent on my apartment was due in just over a week, and I didn't have enough in my checking account to pay it. I'd have to get a job bartending again, and that was the last thing I wanted to do. But there was no shortage of bars in downtown Minneapolis, so it seemed like the most logical option, given the short window. I hated the long drive home at two in the morning, but the tips added up quickly.

I punched the button for the ground floor and set the box on the floor—I had twenty-two floors to descend and didn't care to hold it the whole time. It was warm and stuffy in the elevator, so I grabbed a folder from the box and fanned myself with it.

Ugh, I'd give anything to be naked in front of an industrial fan right now.

And that was all it took, that one single thought, to get me riled up. I suddenly wanted nothing more than to be fucked in that elevator right then and there. I settled for unbuttoning a couple buttons on my blouse—I had already been fired, there was nothing more to lose.

I noticed on the ride up that the elevators had cameras on them, beneath the Plexiglass next to the numbered buttons. I couldn't help but wonder who watched those cameras.

Was someone manning them all the time? Was it security? Or just a recording for safety purposes in case something were to happen? The idea that someone was watching turned me on more than anything, making me wet at the thought. I fluffed my hair, licked my lips, and leaned over to shake my tits in front of the camera, more so for my own entertainment than anyone else's.

When the bell chimed on the ground floor, I picked up my box, making sure to bend over directly in front of the camera. I knew full well that my ass looked good in that skirt and figured someone else might enjoy the view.

Sighing, I made my way out of the building and into the parking lot, annoyed there wasn't even anyone at the security desk for me to wave goodbye to. Nobody gave a shit I had been there.

I reached my car and set my box of crap on the ground while I dug in my purse for the keys, the faint sound of footsteps pounding the pavement behind me.

"Hey! Wait up!"

I turned and saw a man running toward me, his arm waving in the air. It was evident by his attire that he worked security for the building I'd just stormed out of. "Hi," he said once he finally caught up with me. He wiped a bead of sweat from his brow and motioned toward my box. "Can I help you with that?"

"Oh, sure. Thanks, that would be great. It's kinda heavy," I lied.

"I'm Ryan," he said, shoving the box into the backseat of my car and closing the door.

"Alisha. You weren't at the desk," I said, pointing to the building. "When I walked out, I mean. I was gonna say good-bye, but there was no one there."

"Oh, yeah, um. Sorry. I…was distracted."

He stuffed his hands in his pockets and stood there with a gawky expression on his face. "Um, not to make this awkward, but is there any chance you'd like to grab a drink tonight?"

"I don't drink."

"Oh, sure. Yeah, that's cool." I couldn't help but notice the rejection on his face. The poor guy looked defeated and I hadn't even said no to a date, only to the drink. But he gave up so fast I was starting to lose interest.

"Thanks for your help, Ryan." I said finally. He nodded, and we stood there for another uncomfortable second, neither of us making an effort to carry on the conversation. I wasn't in a hurry, but I didn't care to stand there watching the guy sweat either. I was about to reach for the door handle when he spoke up again.

"I saw you," he spit out bashfully. "In, um…in the elevator."

"Oh, my God, I'm so sorry," I feigned innocently. "That was so inappropriate, I—"

"No, no…not at all. I liked it."

"Oh. Oh! Like you *liked it* liked it?"

He nodded, and it was suddenly clear to me why I didn't see him at the desk when I walked out. He must have been preoccupied with concealing a boner.

Yay me!

"I wasn't sure if you knew that we watch…the cameras, I mean. That one feeds to my post."

"I honestly didn't know anyone was watching. I'm sorry, I was—I got fired today. So it was kind of like a 'fuck you' to the guy upstairs, you know?"

"Yeah, sure. That makes sense. Sorry to hear that, though. I guess that means I won't see you around."

I looked at him with new eyes. With his blond hair and light blue eyes, he wasn't unattractive. He wasn't entirely attractive, either. He could stand to gain a few inches in the height department, and his security guard uniform wasn't quite doing it for me either, but something told me he wasn't as inexperienced as he came across.

That maybe he knew a few things.

"So you liked it?" I asked. "What you saw in the elevator?"

"Yeah," he answered a bit too quickly, and I couldn't help but smile. "Come on," I said, taking his hand. "You're going to fuck me in that elevator."

His eyes went wide and he stumbled over his feet as we made our way back to the building, but despite his initial inelegance, Ryan was—at the time—the best fuck I'd ever had.

Called it.

A half-hour later I was back in my car, fixing my hair in the rearview mirror when my phone buzzed from the passenger seat. I recognized the local 7-6-3 area code, but not the number that followed.

A text message.

From an unsaved number.

I'm off at five if you want me to come over and help you change out of that skirt.

Who the hell?

Then a second message.

This is Drew Milner. I figured since I'm no longer your boss...

The man was wearing a wedding ring.

After rolling my eyes, I snapped a quick picture of cleavage, making sure the lace of my bra was showing through my unbuttoned blouse, and sent it to Drew along with an address.

When he showed up at Mrs. Maylen's house around 5:45 that evening, all she could do was laugh. I didn't live there anymore, and it wasn't the first time I intentionally directed a douche bag to the wrong house just to fuck with them. She always got a good laugh out of it, and it wasn't like I was putting her in danger; none of the boner-donors knew we were connected and simply assumed they had the wrong house or quickly figured out they had been played. In this case, it didn't take long for Drew to realize his misfortune.

But the best part was that Mrs. Maylen caught on quickly and slapped a sultry expression on her face—he *was* quite handsome, if I'm being honest—and invited him inside.

She said he couldn't have high-tailed it out of there fast enough, and we laughed about it over dinner for years to come.

SEX KITTEN-LIKE MISTAKES

Alisha

I WAS jobless for over a week, impatient, and waiting to hear back from several bars I had applied to, certain at least one of them would call any day.

Bored and horny, I spent most of that week naked on my couch watching porn on my laptop, nearly picking up the phone to invite Elevator Boy over for a booty call. But when an ad popped up to join a live webcam, I came to the realization that I had been sitting—literally—on a gold mine.

I barely had to do anything to capture Ryan's attention the week before, and he was ready to blow his load before the elevator even reached the main floor. So much so that he followed a complete stranger out to the parking lot and offered to take her to dinner, as if he were interested in anything more than sex.

"You don't belong cooped up in an office anyway," he'd said as we got dressed afterward.

"No? Well, what should I be doing then?"

"Don't take this the wrong way, but…" He shrugged and looked away for a moment, his eyes downcast as he adjusted his belt. "I'd pay to watch what we just did."

"What do you mean?"

"Porn. You should do porn."

His comment threw me off at first. I wasn't about to dive head first into the porn industry, but the more I thought about it, the more enticing it became. I had spent no more than ten minutes in the presence of Drew Milner before he was so turned on he couldn't even introduce me to the rest of the team. And the fact that he was willing to cheat on his wife just for a quick taste?

But I wasn't sure porn was for me, and truth be told, I was afraid to get a glimpse of that world behind the scenes. I didn't want to know enough not to be able to enjoy it anymore. But I needed something more lucrative than bartending, something that would allow me the anonymity I craved and the ability to set my own schedule.

There *was* a job out there for me. And I was looking right at it.

Live girls.

Online.

No one physically there to grope me, shove my hand down their pants, or stick their dick in my ass.

A webcam girl—*that* I could do.

The next day I headed straight to the Ridgedale Mall, ready to invest in my future. Armed with the cash I had set aside for rent, I bought a decent webcam and then headed to the lingerie department.

I was terrible at lingerie, even worse at fashion in general. I lived for a pair of leggings and a good hoodie, and even though I knew I'd end up naked at some point during my lives, I'd have to start out wearing something.

I needed something sexy to entice the viewers, to keep them wanting more so they'd come back. And, to my surprise, after over two hours struggling to find any lingerie that I liked, I managed to make a friend. Apparently when you have no clue how to shop for lingerie, making a friend while standing in line at the checkout counter is a good way to ease the burden; it never hurts to have that second set of eyes.

"You're not wearing that for a man, are you?" the voice behind me asked. He held his hand up to his mouth, almost like he was disgusted, but his eyes told me otherwise.

He was genuinely concerned.

"Excuse me?"

"Sorry, if I may?" He reached for the skimpy garments in my hands, holding them up on full display to get a look at them, clearly oblivious to the customers gawking around us while he analyzed them with intent.

"This is the wrong color for you. Not even a straight man would go for that shit." He shook his head in disappointment and took the remaining items from my arms, setting them on the counter. I couldn't help but stand there looking like an idiot.

"Are you in a hurry?" he asked, not waiting for an answer. He took my arm and pulled me out of the checkout line and back toward the shopping floor. "You can go ahead and restock those, Jen!" he called back to the cashier. She rolled her eyes, and all I could do was offer her a shrug of my shoulders. To my surprise she laughed as I was dragged away, without even a hint of concern for my safety.

"Have fun!" she shouted instead, subsequently moving on to the next customer in line.

"Do you work here or something?" I asked, trying to keep the pace.

"I do, yep. I'm Chris. What's your name, sweetheart?" He held his hand out to me, and despite my reservations, I took it, internally jealous of his ability to talk to strangers as if they were anything but.

"Alisha."

"Ooo, love that name! So pretty." He released my hand and clapped his own together in excitement, turning abruptly and making a beeline to the sexiest of lingerie. "And it just so happens that *you*, my dear, managed to nearly sneak out of here making the biggest sex-kitten-like mistake *ever.*"

"Which is?"

"First of all, nothing says 'trashy' more than a hot pink garter belt." He shuddered, his shoulders shaking as if there were a chill in the air. "You're much too gorgeous for that shit. It's not you, honey, it's him. Don't worry. Just come with me, and we'll get you in something perfect."

We rummaged through the racks, quickly picking through the inventory and avoiding anything similar to the pieces I previously picked out.

"What about this?" I asked, holding up a canary yellow thong and shimming my hips. Chris swiped it out of my hands and tossed it back on the table as my lips formed into a pout.

"Hey, I liked that one," I whined.

"No, you didn't." He shoved another garment in my direction, not bothering to turn and look at me when I took it from his hands, his nose still stuck in the rack.

"Okay, dressing room, here we come!" he finally declared after several minutes of scouring.

"What? No way," I protested.

"Way. Now, scoot!"

"I'm not trying these on for you."

"Calm down, Lisha dear, they're just boobs. Literally *everyone* has seen boobs. But if it makes you feel better, you can keep your panties on since they're already in a bunch anyway." He winked, and my jaw nearly dropped to the floor. But I followed him to the dressing rooms anyway. Because he obviously knew what he was talking about, and for some reason I valued his opinion, despite having just met him.

Caution to the wind, I wiggled out of my clothes and into the first piece of lingerie, Chris standing back and watching as I did so. The piece was snug, but I didn't hate it.

"Push those ta-tas up a bit…there. Yep, there ya go." He stepped back as if admiring his handiwork, grinning like a proud parent. His hands on my shoulders, he turned me so I was facing the floor-length mirror. "Oh, hey, girl!" he said, biting his lip and whistling.

"Wow…"

"Black is really your color! With that skin tone? Do you love it or do you loooove it?"

"I must admit, Chris," I said as I ran my hands down the lacy fabric. "You are excellent at picking out sexy lingerie."

"And don't you forget it!" he said, spinning me to take another look. "What do you need all this for, anyway? It's an awful lot to buy all at once. Oh! Wait! Did you recently lose a ton of weight?" *Gasp.* "Were you fat once?" he whispered, his hand cupped against his mouth. I laughed, despite myself, and shook my head.

"No, I wasn't fat once."

He raised a brow, his head bobbing in wait of my response. And suddenly I wanted nothing more than to tell him. To confide in him like a friend.

I hadn't had one in a long time.

"Okay, fine. I'll tell you. But you can't tell anyone," I said.

"Sweetheart, I don't even know your last name. Who would I tell?"

"Good point. Okay, so…I'm starting a livestream channel. I'm gonna be a webcam girl."

"A webcam girl? As in…like, live nudes or something?" I nodded, biting my lip.

"No…freakin'…way."

"Yes freakin' way."

"Oh, sweetheart…we need to get you some red Louboutin heels!"

———

Two days later I was up and running, live on the web for the first time and doing nothing but cleaning my apartment dressed in a classic French maid outfit, my feather duster sweeping the same surfaces over and over.

My apartment had never been so clean.

Viewers could see and hear me, but I couldn't hear them, not yet anyway. I knew I'd have to invest in some better equipment down the road. It was a mostly PG-13 show those first few times—just a lot of ass cheeks and a few nip slips, but I earned my rent money back within the week.

The following month I was able to pay the landlord on time, and *Lisha's Bedroom* was officially born. Thanks, in part, to my new friend, Chris.

THAT'S WHY I LOOK FAMILIAR

Alisha

WAS it difficult for me to give up promiscuity after meeting Dylan? No. Not at all, actually. I had no issues with monogamy, I just hadn't found anyone I wanted to be monogamous with until I met Dylan, a fact that surprised Kristin, among others. Up until then, my dating life was a continuous list of disappointment, of nights out on the town trying to meet people to take me home and fuck my brains out.

Not that I walked around with a sign around my neck saying that, but the conquests were harder to come by than you might think.

When you're the only sober one in a bar full of drunk people, it's hard to see past the idiocy that can ensue. They're the ones sporting beer goggles, not me, so for them it's a win-win.

The trick was to find someone just sober enough not to be sloppy.

Nonetheless, the website helped redirect my interests. I was so busy I didn't *need* to date. Not to mention, I could call up a private session at any time and get my rocks off that way. In the beginning, I worked every day of the week. Until I no longer needed to.

But every night was something different. I loved the change of pace, the element of surprise in never really knowing what I'd get.

Private sessions quickly become a lucrative favorite. I didn't need to stream for hours on end once I started booking private sessions.

And I'd gained some regulars.

Most enjoyable were the ones I would consider straight-laced men. The ones that required little to no prep in terms of hair, makeup, and wardrobe. My first private session was awkward though, to say the least.

I dressed in a silk black robe and my signature red stiletto heels, my nipples poking through the thin fabric perfectly. I kept the thermostat low for just that reason.

My customer had a girl-next-door fantasy—a lot of them did, actually. In my experience, most men were under the impression the perfect girl-next-door was a freak in the sheets, dressing in sexy lingerie under their conservative clothes, just desperate for someone to notice.

The misconception always made me chuckle.

For this particular customer, however, I was asked to have my hair done and wear a little makeup. His "neighbor" was supposed to be getting ready for a night on the town. She would enter the bedroom, having just done her hair and makeup, and drop her robe, exposing her naked body for him to secretly admire through her bedroom window.

I straightened my hair, my face highlighted, along with a touch of bronzer and a layer of mascara. The finishing touch was the colorless lip gloss he was adamant about—as if red lipstick would have taken away the character's innocence. I turned on the camera and stood in front of it, giving him a moment to admire the view.

"Mm, yes. You are looking lovely today, Willow," he said, using his desired name for me. His camera pointed straight to his crotch, never his face—you'd be surprised how many of them are—his dick hard as he stroked it with his right hand. I couldn't tell if he was married—another hazard of the right-handed man. "Show me the back," he commanded.

I turned and bent slightly, showing off my plump derriere. He moaned and pumped a little faster.

I hadn't even taken off my robe yet.

He narrated the scene out loud, as if reading from a script. "I'm watching you through your window, Willow. It's dark outside, the breeze is blowing in and it's chilly. Are you cold?"

I slowly untied the robe, letting it fall from my shoulders, the fabric soft when it grazed my nipples. I shivered, feeling the draft, the goosebumps forming on my breasts. I played coy, my fingers raking through a rack of clothes as I stood there naked, trying to decide what to wear. All the while, I feigned ignorance of the camera, never once looking over at it.

Ope, silly me. I seem to have dropped a hanger on the ground. I better bend over and pick it up.

I hear it then, the sound of his balls slapping against his leg, against his hand. He jerks off violently, the sight of me bent over—my ass and pussy on full display for him—seemingly what he'd been hoping to see.

He clicks off without another word.

The session cost him nearly a hundred dollars.

After a quick shower, I threw on a jacket, grabbed my purse and headed out the door. I was on a bit of a high from the excitement of my website taking off, but I was bored. I needed a change of scenery and a basket of wings, so I shot Chris a text and asked him to meet me at Thirsty's on the off-chance he was free.

Once inside, I claimed a seat at the bar, the bartender approaching a moment later with a friendly but harmless smile on his face. He seemed more like Chris's type than mine.

"What can I get ya?" he asked, setting a cocktail napkin in front of me.

"Just a Shirley Temple, and a basket of honey barbecue wings, please."

"Coming right up."

The gawker spotted me within minutes, his big brown eyes drinking me in. Despite my lack of interest, I couldn't help but admire his stature, the muscles in his forearm. He sipped his drink before standing and making his way over to me.

"Hi," he said to my surprise. No one-liner. No wink. It was unusual, the lack of originality in his game. I nodded and turned back to the TV behind the bar, the local news informing me of yet another shooting in Minneapolis.

"I'm Jacob." He stuck his hand out in my direction, holding it there and waiting for me to take it. I had dated plenty of men like him. Men who think they're God's gift to women, that they're some kind of rare breed. Spoiler alert: they're not. There's one on just about every corner.

But I liked his hair. The salt and pepper look worked for him. The thought to run my fingers through it danced in my mind, but I knew better than to touch him. Touching led to kissing, which led to fucking, and that inevitably led to disappointment.

I'd had enough disappointment.

I was turning over a new leaf, and wanted to eat my damn wings in peace. "Can I buy you a drink?" Jacob asked, taking his rejected hand back and stuffing it in his coat pocket.

"No, thank you, I don't drink."

"Then what are you doing at a bar?"

"They have good wings."

He chuckled, and it brought out the crow's feet around his eyes. When he smiled, he was more handsome than I originally thought, but for some reason, he reminded me of Vincent, the guy I fooled around with for a while after high school.

Our last night together was the first and only time I drank alcohol. We had been seeing each other for a couple weeks, which at eighteen really only meant we were learning new sex positions, but definitions aside, two weeks with a guy was considered a long time for me, even back then.

Attachments weren't my thing.

We were fresh out of high school, and the summer was just getting started. I was on the hunt for a job, and Mrs. Maylen worked weekdays, so Monday through Friday I did little more than hang around the house, bored out of my mind.

I hadn't really dealt with the loss of my mother, though it wasn't like I had deemed it as such. I didn't *lose* her; I knew exactly where she was.

Buried.

Her corpse rotting in the ground of a donated cemetery plot.

Because she chose drugs and alcohol over me. Over her own daughter.

And for some reason, I spilled my guts about this to Vincent. His hair-brained idea was that all I needed was a good fuck and a bottle of vodka. "Numb the pain, just like she did," he had said.

So I did.

I took his advice, and together we got shit-faced drunk. I giggled all night, and danced naked on the coffee table in his living room. We took body shots off one another and he prank-called his buddies while I made sex noises in the background.

But as fun as it was, his master plan failed.

The next morning I woke up sore between my legs and more exhausted than I'd been when I'd laid down the night before. My head throbbed, and I rubbed at my temples. I had no choice but pry my eyes open and squint at the sunlight that seeped in through the curtains. I wanted to move, to get out of his bed and go home, but my stomach gurgled with the threat of vomit, so I stayed.

He lay there beside me, naked and lying on his stomach, his bare ass exposed to the elements. I looked under the covers to find that I was naked too. I remembered very little. Limbs pressed together, mouths on mouths, his limp dick in my hand. "Whiskey dick," he had said when the appendage failed him during round two.

He hadn't even been drinking whiskey, so it made no sense to me at the time. How was I to know it was a universal term?

I didn't understand the appeal of alcohol, the desire to repeat the cycle over and over, day in and day out. It didn't even taste good. I knew then that I'd never drink again, out of spite for my mom, if anything.

But mostly because I simply didn't want to.

. . .

"You look so familiar," Jacob said, pulling me back to the present, to the game-less stranger doing his best to impress a girl who just wanted to stuff her face with chicken wings. I sipped my drink and twirled the ice with my straw.

"Yeah? How so?"

"I don't know. I just feel like I've seen you before. Although, I don't know how I'd forget a face like yours."

"That's what they all say, Jacob."

"Oh. Wow, I'm so sorry. This must happen to you all the time."

"What's that?"

"Weird men hitting on you in bars."

"It does," I acknowledged coolly before turning to my phone. Chris had texted. Jacob pulled his wallet from his back pocket, removed a twenty and dropped it onto the bar. I knew he was about to leave, to take the hint and buzz off. And if I'm being honest, a small part of me wanted to let him take me home—I was oddly intrigued by him.

But the wedding band on his left hand was a turn off.

Men like him were part of the reason I was single in the first place. "*Lisha's Bedroom*," I said.

"Excuse me?"

"That's why I look familiar." I stood and grabbed my jacket from the back of the chair. His face fell in shame when recognition finally hit him. "Go home to your wife," I said, sauntering out the door and raising my phone to my ear.

"Hello?"

"Christopher…"

"Oh, God, what did I do now?"

"Nothing, I just like to freak you out."

"Well, stop it! It always makes me feel like I'm in trouble when you call me Christopher. What can I do ya for, lovely?"

"Ice cream. Bring me ice cream. I'll queue up *The Real Housewives*-of-Wherever-the-Fuck-They-Live-Now."

"Ooh, you're always so salty. I love it. See you in twenty!"

Until I met Dylan, Chris was the one and only reliable man in my life. The fact that he was gay and never tried to get into my pants made him easy to love.

YOU CAN'T FIX STUPID

Dylan

Did the website bother me?

Of course.

What kind of man would I be if it didn't?

But what could I have done? Alisha started that website long before she met me, and I sure as shit didn't deserve a say in whether or not she kept it up and running. My wife had a mind of her own, and she didn't hesitate to use it. She was a grown woman, fully capable of making her own decisions. That's not to say I always agreed with her, especially when it came to that damn website.

It did mean, however, that I had to figure out a way to help her. She deserved more than what *Lisha's Bedroom* offered her. Sure, the money was great, but she was already set for life by the time I met her. She didn't *need* to work anymore, she just wanted to.

So, did I ask her to shut it down? Eventually, yes. In the early days while I was busy making sure she fell in love with me and stayed there? Nope. Not a fucking chance.

She bored easily. She demanded more out of life than the average person, and when she was working, when she was performing for her customers, she was thriving. It boosted her self-esteem, her confidence. It also put money in her bank account, and after a lifetime of poverty, how could she turn that down? How could she stop once she started?

Alisha spent her life under scrutiny, being judged for her lack of wealth and her sexuality. I wasn't there to see it then, but I'd heard stories, mostly from my grandmother, but even Alisha slipped in the occasional admission every once in a while. Like the time she was asked to leave a local boutique because employees saw the backpack she carried that doubled as a purse and assumed she was there to shoplift.

Or when a theater attendant asked her to leave in the middle of *Titanic* because he thought she had sneaked in, even though she presented a ticket stub for the right date, time, and movie.

Residents in the small town she grew up in knew her. They knew her mother, Darlene, and her history with substance abuse. They made the assumption that Alisha was no different, that she'd grow up and follow the same path, stepping directly into the very footprints her mother had laid out for her.

But once she had wealth? Once they knew she wasn't an addict, that she didn't enter a store with the intent to steal? Everything changed for her.

She didn't, though; she never changed who she was to meet the demands of society. She lived her life unapologetically, because that's how she deserved to live it.

She radiated confidence, and it transpired into the bedroom, into her web show, and her customers couldn't get enough of it. They couldn't get enough of *her*.

Somehow, she even managed to keep her profession under wraps around town. Most of the locals had no clue how she'd dug herself out of poverty. And she liked it that way, the anonymity. She deserved it after everything she'd been through.

Until I was murdered and it all went to shit.

After that everybody knew our business—everybody knew *her* business. She had been exposed, and they were fascinated by it—by *her*.

And the funny thing about that? She had gotten out of the business by that time. Yet it was the first thing the media picked up on, the first thing they pounced on as soon as the investigation began.

America ate that shit right up.

Men were enamored with her, and women hated her *because* the men were enamored with her—although, some of them secretly loved her, too. It didn't matter that she had retired from the industry. To them, she was still Lisha. She was nothing more than a porn star, and that's all she'd ever be.

She became a household name and every teen boy's wet dream.

If I weren't dead, I'd be on my soap box every single day trying to show those fuckers who she really is. But here's the thing: you can't fix stupid. You can't change someone's mind when they're set on believing a misguided truth. I mean, that's the whole premise of politics, right? Nobody ever switches sides; we're all either Republicans or Democrats until the end. That's it, that's all.

The same goes for life, really. Most people don't get a second chance to make a first impression.

And when it comes to Alisha, as she's always said, you're either with her or against her.

KYLE IS A DOUCHE

Alisha

I MEET with Kyle at 10:00 a.m. every Tuesday. Sometimes Thursdays, too, depending on the week. He tells me we'll meet more frequently as the trial draws nearer, which is fine. It's nice to sit and chat with a man from time to time; the women in this place are so fucking catty.

But Kyle's kind of a douche, too, so I'm not sure which is worse. And today it seems both Kyle and I are in a mood, which is never a good thing.

I know this meeting isn't going to end well before it even starts, and while I brace myself for impact, Kyle unpacks the contents of his briefcase. I take a seat across from him at the table and watch as he opens several folders and spreads their contents out. The paperwork seems to have multiplied since the last time he was here.

He finally stops pulling shit out of his briefcase, and looks up at me, leaning over the table and lacing his hands together as if he has something important to tell me. "Hey," is all he says.

"Hi."

"How are you holding up?"

"Fine."

He looks as if he's about to explode, and we haven't even started talking about my case yet. I can't say I feel any differently—tensions have been high between us for weeks—but you'd think my thousand-dollar-an-hour attorney would be able to keep his shit together—or at least fake it well enough to make me believe he knows what the hell he's doing.

I can't help but hold my breath in anticipation of what he's uncovered since his last visit.

"Look, here's the deal, Alisha. We need to go over a few things." He shuffles through one of the folders and pulls out a newspaper clipping. When he slides it across the table, his uses his sausage finger to point at the provocative photo of me. "*This* is what the media thinks of you. What the public sees."

Personally, I find the photo quite flattering, but I shrug and cross my arms, leaning back in the chair and not caring for his tone. "And?" I ask.

"And what?"

"What's the problem?"

"Really? I show you a nearly nude photo of yourself— that made the front page of the *Star Tribune*, mind you—and *that's* your response?"

"It's no secret what I do for a living."

"No, it's not. And that's part of the problem."

"I'm not ashamed of my profession, Kyle."

"Great. By all means, be *proud* of the so-called *work* that you do. But get this through your head. You're a porn star. And the media knows it. The general public knows it, too.

And juries? Juries have little to no sympathy for sex workers. So you're fucked at the gate, and not the way you like it. They'll form an opinion of you before the DA even finishes his opening statement. Do you get what I'm saying to you?"

"None of that should matter, considering I didn't do this. I didn't kill him, Kyle."

He sighs and turns back to his paperwork. I see the frustration in his eyes, in the way his lip turns up when he doesn't hear the answer he wants to hear. I know he's trying.

But he needs to try harder.

"The evidence is bigger than you think. It's stacked. There's not much to work with in terms of a defense. Our best shot? To create reasonable doubt. You really haven't given me anything that will allow me to do more than that."

I nod, despite myself. I don't want to accept this, his assumption that a jury can't see past sexuality to find a semblance of innocence. But his words hold weight. There's truth behind them, whether I like it or not.

"Let's go over the morning of again," he says, as if it's only the second time we've discussed it and not the fourteen-hundredth.

"Why?" I ask, annoyed again and rolling my eyes.

"Because I still don't understand it."

"You're a well-educated attorney, Kyle. What's not to understand?"

He pulls a face and twists his mouth into a tight grin. I can practically see the smoke coming from his ears. "Enlighten me."

"Fine. Cliff notes, then." I lean forward on the table, getting real close to Kyle and doing my best to match his demeanor. "I woke up. I peed. I brushed my teeth. I went for a run. I came home. My husband was dead. I puked. I pulled the knife out of his chest. Police busted through my door before I even understood what was happening. They brought me to the county jail, fed me cardboard, and delayed my phone call. Then, *magically,* two days later"—I smile as if this is the best part of the story—"I got to meet *you.*"

"You're charming as usual, Alisha. Anyone ever tell ya that?"

I lean back in the plastic chair as Kyle runs his hands over his thinning scalp. I think of Dylan's full head of hair and suddenly wish I could run my fingers through it. I miss the scent of his shampoo. "Tell it again," he says.

"What?"

"Tell it again."

"Why?"

"Fill in the margins for me…no more abstracts."

"Fuck this, Kyle! No. All that matters is that I didn't kill my husband!"

"No? What if you blacked out? Do you drink?"

"No."

"How's your mental health? Before all this, I mean…"

"I didn't black out." I say through gritted teeth. "And I'm not fucking crazy." He shrugs with nonchalance, as if he doesn't believe that either.

"You said the two of you argued the night before. What about?"

"I already told you I didn't want to talk about that."

"No? Well, I do. Tell me what you argued about."

"No."

He slams his hand down on the table, the pen jumping up like a popcorn kernel. "Here's the thing, Alisha. I think you *did* kill your husband. I think you stabbed him repeatedly until he bled out. And then you got caught. Does that matter? No. Does it change the fact that I'm here, representing you to the best of my ability? No." He points a chubby finger in my direction. It's much less threatening than he thinks. "But it does mean that you don't get to sit here and fucking lie to me anymore. Tell. Me. What. Happened."

"Fuck you, Kyle!" I hiss.

After a moment of silence and an intense stare down, Kyle stands and starts shoving paperwork back into his brief-case. My heart rate increases at the realization that he's about to walk out on me. He may even quit.

I'd have to start all over with someone new.

And there's no time for that.

"What are you doing?" I ask quietly.

"Leaving. I have other clients to see. Clients who actually give me the information I need to represent them in a court of law."

They hurt, his words. The memory of what I've lost. All of it just fucking hurts. And it's taken too long for me to realize that Kyle's right. If I have any shot in hell of getting out of here, I have to tell him everything.

But I'm not sure I can do that.

THE MASKS WE WEAR

Alisha

ALL THIS TRIAL prep is killing me.

I can't take it—Kyle's insistence that I "practice" looking at the crime scene photos, his need to walk through every minute of that day over and over, even though there's no possible way I could share something about it he doesn't already know. Yet, it's the first thing he asks me every time I see him. *"Walk me through the day of the murder,"* he always says.

And even though I know it's coming, I fight the urge to stab a pen through his eye every time.

I'm worn out, my patience is thin and soon to be nonexistent, but every visit from Kyle means the trial is getting closer. I'm either reaching the end or approaching the brink of darkness, should I end up with life in prison. That thought is terrifying. That part makes me want to crawl into a hole and die. I need to get the fuck out of here.

I'm not sure if that will ever happen.

So I go through the motions. I appease Kyle and—with a good amount of attitude—I answer his questions. I try to fill in the gaps so he can use them to poke holes in the prosecution's case.

Today is no different than last week, except we're opening a brand new can of worms. One I hadn't expected to tap into, yet here we are. Why I ever thought I could keep anything from my attorney is beyond me; he always knows, and if he doesn't yet, he will find out.

"Why didn't you tell me about your court-appointed therapy with Dr. Lindsay?" he asks, massaging his temples. Only two days have passed since we last met, and already he's managed to dig up more dirt on me.

I can only imagine what the state has found.

"Kristin? Why does that matter?"

"Why *wouldn't* that matter? It's public record, and you didn't think to tell me?"

I shrug, mentally unprepared to discuss anything to do with Kristin. I nearly ask about patient confidentiality before it occurs to me that she could be asked to testify.

"Has she turned up on the witness list?" I ask with an upturned brow.

"What happened that got you sent to her office?"

"Has she?"

"Yes."

Fuck.

"It wasn't just one thing…but none of it was my fault."

"Right," he drawls. "Continue…"

The first time I met with Dr. Kristin Lindsay, my mind raced as I tried to make sense of why I was in her office to begin

SHANNON JUMP

with. I didn't choose to be there. I didn't voluntarily sign up. And while I'd done everything to fight it, there I sat, pissed off and ready to argue with a complete stranger about why I am the way I am and how I didn't deserve to be there.

But as irritated as I was, I couldn't get over how good it smelled in that office. Like lavender and vanilla and chamomile or something to that effect. An array of essential oils meant to calm my nerves, strategically fermenting in the room for no purpose other than to trick me into relaxation so I'd spill all my secrets.

I wanted that smell. I needed it, craved it to the point where I hopped online the second I got home and ordered enough of it to supply a small country.

And the fucked up thing is that I never used the oils. All they did was remind me of Kristin and that damn office I could never get out of fast enough.

And the reason I had to go there in the first place? Complete and utter bullshit, although I seem to be the only one who thinks so. I'd run into a client at a coffee shop. It was rare, but it did happen from time to time. And this particular client had a thing for submissive women. During our cam sessions, he liked to put me in my place, to give instructions I didn't particularly care to follow, and my refusal to do so only turned him on more.

He was the kind of man every woman steers clear of in the real world, and as luck would have it, he was standing right next to me.

"Lisha!" he beamed, a shit-eating grin on his face as if we went way back, as if we'd ever met in person.

Brenner Dixon.

I smiled, my own camera-ready grin always in my back pocket and ready for use at any given moment, despite my growing lack of people skills. "That's me," I admitted, raising a finger to my lips to quiet him. "But let's keep that between us." Why I didn't think to feign complete ignorance is beyond me.

I should have excused myself and walked away, pretended like I didn't know who he was and there was no way he could possibly know me.

But I suppose once someone's seen every inch of you, it only gets harder to conceal your identity.

Brenner winked like he was in on something, leaning in and placing a hand on the small of my back. "I do love a good secret," he said. "In fact, why don't we head to the bathroom and share one of our own?"

Two seconds.

That's about how long it took for Brenner to proposition me in public for the first time.

But I wasn't one to mix business with pleasure, especially with locals, and my only intention was to let him down gently, grab my coffee, and be on my merry way. "I'm sorry, I'm actually in a bit of a hurry."

"Hmm, playing hard to get, huh? I like it."

"No, I'm not actually," I corrected him. "I really do have somewhere to be." I didn't, but that fact was none of his business. I had a right to refuse his services without reason.

"Tight pussy like yours? Trust me, it'll be quick. Let's go." He took hold of my forearm and pulled me in the direction of the bathroom.

"I said no," I snapped, yanking my arm from his grasp.

"Fucking bitch," he hissed, reaching for me again. His fingers were rough as they dug into my skin. Fortunately for me, I'm left handed, and he'd taken hold of the wrong arm. I took a swing before he had a chance to take another step.

Brenner ended up with a broken nose.

And then gifted me with assault charges.

Which led to court-ordered anger management, despite the fact that I was the one who'd been sexually harassed. The punishment for him failed to stretch beyond the bill he received from his lawyer.

After that, he did everything he could to trash my name in the forums, but it did nothing to harm my career. If anything, I gained clientele. Nobody in those forums gave a shit, they just wanted a show.

And that's what I continued to give them.

But my run-in with Brenner wasn't my only offense. A couple months later, I met an angry housewife. The woman—a mother of three, and honorary neighborhood soccer mom, slash chauffeur—claimed her husband was cheating on her.

With me.

Because he subscribed to my channel, which she'd caught him jacking off to by way of a nanny cam strategically hidden in their bedroom.

Apparently that's considered cheating by some standards, though I'd never seen the man face-to-face. What I learned that afternoon is that oranges make great weapons.

But a wife scorned makes an even greater one.

And as was my luck, her husband happened to work at a law firm, and the fact that I'd pitched an orange at her face, hitting her square in the jaw, made me the perpetrator once again.

And sent me straight to court-ordered therapy on account of my "rage."

On that first day in Kristin's office, our intake session, I claimed residence on the love seat, and she looked at me with expectant eyes. I presented as a confident woman, one who knows her shit stinks but isn't bothered by the fact.

Everyone's shit stinks.

"Good morning, Alisha. I'm Dr. Kristin Lindsay, but you can call me Kristin. I'm proud of you for coming in today." She took a seat in an executive leather chair across from me. She was petite, wearing black trousers and a button-up that was so tight I found myself wondering if it was intentionally snug or perhaps she'd recently put on some weight. Why the thought crossed my mind, I wasn't sure, but I brushed it aside and nodded, saying nothing in response to her introduction. I was there to answer her questions, not to offer up information on my own free will.

"I thought we'd start by getting to know each other a bit. Does that work for you?"

"Sure."

"What brings you in today? Let's pick at the scab, so to speak," she said, smirking at the cleverness of her analogy. I didn't find it as clever as she did and instead wondered how often she used it with new clients, playing it off as she'd said it for the first time.

Already I sensed her judgment of me. I felt it in the way she studied me, my mannerisms and reactions. I heard it in her tone, the condescension and vague introduction—like she didn't want to be there with me any more than I wanted to be there with her. In her profession, she was supposed to be a neutral party. She was supposed to be Switzerland against the world.

But we were both guilty, she and I.

I didn't care for her either.

So I guess that means I judged her a little, too. She came off weak, but in control. Confident in an unfamiliar way—as if her confidence only resided on the outside. As if she, too, wore a mask.

"I'm required to be here." I replied to her question. She looked at the page of notes in her lap, pulling her glasses down her nose. I wondered if they were just for show or if she actually needed them.

"Yes, it says here you received a court order."

"Right. So, that's why I'm here. Some asshole in a choir robe told me I had to be."

She pulled a face, and it was evident my response wasn't what she'd expected. She looked disappointed, as if she knew me well enough to be disappointed in me.

"I don't think that's a very constructive comment. Do you?"

"Nope."

"Let's start over then. What brings you in today?" she asked again, and all I could do was outwardly sigh. I'd met my match, and I wasn't sure what to make of that. But appease her I did, because what else were we going to do for the next hour?

"So, that's it?" Kyle asks when I finish.

"That's it."

"How often did you see her?"

"Weekly. Until I came here."

"And how are you doing? With the, uh…the addiction."

I scoff at the fact that Kyle suddenly thinks he understands me, that he discovered my sex addiction diagnosis without my consent. I don't feed into his concern. Instead, I look him in the eye, teasing him with a smirk and an unsolicited air kiss. "Everyone has a vice, Kyle. Even you, I'm sure."

"Right. I'll see ya in a couple days," he says, picking up his briefcase. He stands, his chair knocking against the wall behind him.

"That's it?"

"For today, yes."

And I almost want to cry.

The clock ticks loudly on the wall above the door, and as much as I don't want to look over at it, I do. I don't want to shoot the shit with Kyle longer than necessary, but I'd rather be in here with him, talking myself out of propositioning him with a blow job, than back in the pod.

But back to the pod I go.

Because this time, Kyle doesn't sit back down.

HOW'S THE WIFE?

Dylan

I WARNED Alisha that her career choice would come back to bite her in the ass one day. All those men, and even the women she entertained, whom she had essentially teased during her days with *Lisha's Bedroom*, were bound to grow angry at some point. They were bound to lash out and find ways to take claim to Alisha.

Everyone wants what they can't have.

Not that I was an expert on the subject, but her run-ins with that asshole, Brenner, and that other schmuck's angry wife were proof that jealousy can spark anywhere, even in a virtual environment. The majority of her customers were ignorant enough to believe they were the only ones—that Alisha performed exclusively for them.

It was no surprise they were obsessed with her; it was easy to fall under her spell, especially if you took her personality out of it and focused on her physical attributes. But none of them knew her the way I did. They only knew the side of her that she presented to them, the character she portrayed on screen.

When we met, she told me she was an actress. Which I suppose is accurate, although somewhat misleading. I knew what she did for a living, though. I knew Alisha worked in the porn industry. I just wanted her to be the one to tell me.

And she did, after a few days.

Not that I ever admitted I'd known all along.

I mean, I benefited from it, too. I loved to watch her perform for the camera, to touch herself in ways any man would blow a load over. It worked for us for a while. She pleasured herself with her toys, viewers paid money to watch her in a private session, and I dove in tongue first to finish the job when the cameras went off.

The fact that none of them were able to touch her made the pill of jealousy a little easier to swallow, and eventually I didn't think much of it anymore.

Until the strange phone calls started coming. Her number was unlisted—for obvious reasons—so it was clear someone was desperate to track her down and had succeeded in doing so. She had to change her number because the calls were coming so frequently.

"You're making a big deal out of nothing," she said when I expressed concern for the umpteenth time. It was a Friday morning, and I was exhausted from a long week of showing houses, but the conversation needed to be had. The coffeemaker beeped, and I poured its contents into a travel mug, topping it off with cream and sugar. I'd debated playing hooky for the day, but I'd been doing that more often than I cared to admit and needed to get back into the swing of things. I wanted Alisha to shut down the site; in my opinion, it had run its course and was turning into nothing but a nuisance.

Plus, I was gearing up to address the topic of a baby. I had no fucking clue how *that* would go over with Alisha, but I did know I didn't want my future child's mom working in porn. Sharing her with anyone—virtually or otherwise—would no longer be an option once that seed was planted.

"No, I'm not," I said, twisting the lid onto the tumbler and turning to her. She looked beautiful in one of my white T-shirts, her bare legs exposed. I stifled a groan and watched a smirk form on her lips; she knew what those legs did to me, how they shot a current straight to my dick just at the sight of them. I felt the friction against my pants as she hopped off the counter and pulled the shirt over her head, the perfect mounds of her breasts on full display, her nipples perky in the chilly room. I couldn't help but stare. I was putty in her hands, and she knew it. Without another thought, I abandoned my coffee on the counter to ravish my wife. She needed my cock just as I needed her pussy.

And I'd fuck her ten ways to Sunday if she asked me to.

It wasn't until later that morning, after I'd showered for the second time, that I realized Alisha had played me again. She didn't approve of our topic of conversation.

Husband wants to discuss your poor career choice? No problem! Let's distract him with sex, and he'll forget what he was talking about in the first place. Ready, set, go!

I made a mental note to table the discussion for later. It wasn't over.

On my way in to work I found a parking space at Caribou Coffee because, in my haste to love on my wife, I forgot my coffee on the kitchen counter, and I was officially overdue for a caffeine fix.

I pulled open the door to the lobby, stopping dead in my tracks as I took in the face in front of me.

My stepbrother, Sawyer, who stood just as motionless, his fingers wrapped around a to-go cup of coffee.

I hadn't spoken to the sorry excuse for a man in years, on account of him sleeping with girlfriend, Ivy. The two of them shared similar interests, and at the time, I was working a lot, trying to make a living and saving for a ring. So, like a careless idiot, I suggested they hang out. I sent Sawyer in my place when I couldn't attend an Aerosmith concert with her. I subbed him in for our bowling league when I was busy with a closing that resulted in a huge commission. So, I didn't question it when they started making plans without me.

Really, I was just a sucker and fell for the whole we're-just-friends bullshit, I trusted my brother. And I trusted Ivy even more. Sure, I should have found it weird that my own brother was growing so close with my girlfriend, but truthfully? I barely had the time to notice.

Until I walked in on them fucking.

In *my* apartment. On *my* couch.

Last I heard they were separated and he was living somewhere in the Twin Cities. Why Sawyer's ugly mug was standing in a coffee shop in the middle of fucking nowhere was beyond me.

"Hey, man," he said when he spotted me. He looked about as confused as I felt, but he was the one out of place there. Not me.

"I have nothing to say to you." I shoved past him and made my way to the counter, confident he didn't have the balls to try another hand at conversation.

I was wrong.

The sound of his voice felt like a knife to my back.

"Come on, Dylan, don't be that way. It's been long enough, don't you think?"

"Has it? How's the wife?"

"Okay, you know what? I don't need this shit. Yes, I married Ivy. I'm sorry I slept with your girlfriend and ended up happy. For a while, anyway, but she's gone now. So, fuck you, man! You're married, too, remember? And from what I hear, you're pretty damn happy with *your* wife. At some point, I'd like to think you'd get over it!" He pivoted and walked out the door, punching the air—or fist-fighting a mosquito, who knows—once he stepped outside.

Several sets of eyes bore into me as I watched my brother stomp off. For a second, I debated leaving too, but I wasn't about to forgo my morning coffee a third time. I stepped up to the counter, ignoring the prying eyes, and placed my order, nearly convincing myself to call it a day and head back home.

I found Sawyer in the parking lot on the way out. Apparently he hadn't had enough yet.

To my surprise, the words out of his mouth were, "I'm sorry." He shook his head, almost in disbelief, and I saw it then—the regret in his eyes. The knowledge that what he took from me could never be returned, gift receipt or not.

I didn't want Ivy anymore, but I couldn't forgive my brother either.

"I know, man. I know," I said. With a turn of the heel, I headed off in the direction of my car, ultimately deciding to go straight home. The day was shot anyway.

"That's it?"

"What's it?"

"I say I'm sorry and you just hop back in your car and leave?"

"I don't have time for this today," I said with a sigh,

despite the fact I was about to head home and sit in front of the TV.

"No, of course you don't. Just like you didn't have time for Ivy back *then*."

At lightning speed, I slammed my coffee to the ground and clocked Sawyer in the jaw before I had a second to reconsider my actions.

The reflex was unexpected; I wasn't really the fighting kind.

He stumbled and brought a hand to his mouth, dabbing at the blood that dripped from his bottom lip. I thought he'd fight back, at least throw a punch or two.

But he didn't, the coward.

Instead he backed off without another word. I didn't even bother to watch him walk away.

It was the last time I ever saw my brother.

Why I couldn't let it go is beyond me. Did I still love Ivy? No. But that wasn't the point. The point was that my brother, the one person I was supposed to be able to trust, betrayed me.

Loyalties may run thick, but so does bullshit.

And no one wants to step in that.

AFTER-SEX SNUGGLES

Dylan

YOU KNOW THAT PHRASE, "you never know what you've got 'til it's gone?" I never knew I wanted to be a father, how much I wanted to start a family with Alisha. I thought it would always be just us. Kids were never really on our radar—at least not in the beginning. We were enamored with one another, and nothing else mattered for the longest time.

Until it did.

Part of me wants to admit it took some convincing for Alisha to realize she wanted a baby, too. But in my heart, I knew better. She wanted a baby, and she always had. She just couldn't admit it to herself.

The first time the conversation came up, we had just made love—Alisha hated it when I called it that—and even though she wasn't a fan of after-sex snuggles, she let me hold her. We always joked that our roles were reversed, but it never bother me. I knew I wasn't less of a man just because I wanted to cuddle with my wife.

"Do you ever think about having kids?" I asked her. I felt her body tense in response; of course, she tried to hide it, but I felt it when every muscle in her body tightened and her heart rate increased.

"I can't," she said after a minute. I didn't know what that meant; whether she physically couldn't because of some medical reason or if it was emotional. Something in her psyche that told her she couldn't be a mother.

"What do you mean?" I asked, running my fingers softly up and down her arm.

"I just...I don't think I could do it."

"Oh, babe...I know you could. You'd be a great mother." She pulled away from me and sat up, pulling the sheet over her chest to cover her breasts.

"Is that what you want? Kids?"

"Well, of course. You don't?"

"No. But hear me out. I know I'm *supposed* to want kids. To dream of babies and shitty diapers and nursing until my nipples are raw. But I don't. I don't want that, because..." She paused, as if the words were foreign on her tongue, their taste bitter. I squeezed her hand, my fingers laced between hers. "I don't want to turn out like her," she nearly whispered.

"Like your mother? Alisha, you are *not* your mother."

"I know that. But the potential is there. It's always there."

"Baby, come on. I know you. You'll never be her."

"No, I won't. But that doesn't mean I'll be a good mom. My career alone should tell you that. How is that fair to our child, Dylan?"

"You'll have to quit eventually, right?"

"Right. But the internet won't. It will always be there."

"So? You changed your last name when we got married;

the business is set up under Hill. How would anyone ever know? Just think about it. Somewhere, deep down, I think your heart feels the same way."

And it did.

After that we played fast and loose with condoms, and Alisha's IUD expired a few weeks later. So, I knew she wanted a kid; she wouldn't have let her IUD expire if she didn't.

When she got pregnant, those double lines suddenly became everything. We were excited, and nervous. Her anticipation was palpable. But neither of us had a fucking clue what we were doing.

THERE'S NO MUSIC

Alisha

I WASN'T sure why Dylan never went to work that morning, the morning of his caffeine-less nightmare. I didn't ask. I figured he'd tell me if he wanted to, and he never did offer up a reason.

I did see the blood on his knuckles, however.

Nonetheless, we spent the day binge-watching Netflix and eating junk food. Neither of us were expecting company, but the doorbell rang anyway.

And there it was, another gift with my name on it.

An edible arrangement from my apparent secret admirer.

"Maybe it's time to give up the website...shut it down a little earlier than we planned." Dylan suggested, his hands massaging my shoulders and sending shivers down my spine.

"You're distracting me with words again," I muttered in a daze. I was under his spell; the heat of his touch seemed to do that to me.

"We don't need the money," he reminded me.

"I know."

"So why don't you just shut it down? Let me have you all to myself." I didn't disagree with his logic, but I wasn't afraid to let him sweat it out a bit either. Give him a chance to think he had some convincing to do.

He didn't.

And the truth is, I'd already made the decision to shut it down earlier that morning. I was ready to hang up all the sexy lingerie and save it for a rainy day. "Is somebody jealous?" I teased anyway.

"Yes," he said with raw conviction. My head shot up from his chest at the unexpected admission. I brought a hand to Dylan's cheek, the desperation in his eyes nearly enough to bring a tear to my own. "Baby, I…I'm so sorry," I said.

"You didn't know, I get it."

"No, I didn't…I didn't know it bothered you. Why didn't you tell me?"

"I wanted it to be your decision. But I don't want to share you anymore, Alisha. I'm ready to have you all to myself."

"No, you're absolutely right. I'll shut it down tomorrow and refund the unused credits. I'll dissolve the business."

"Really? Just like that?" I smiled at the shock on his face.

"Just like that," I confirmed.

"Wow, I kind of expected an argument there." He pulled me close as his lips curled into a smile.

"It's time. I'm almost embarrassed to admit it, but I think I've grown out of it. All the dressing up and make-believe role play is getting old. Now I can sit around in sweat pants!" I pecked a kiss onto his cheek, amused at his attempt not to smile.

"Wow, you're really giving me something to look forward to in this marriage," he teased, and I playfully shoved him.

"You know what I mean! Plus, it's not like I'm getting rid of the toys…who says we can't still enjoy those?"

"I do like the sound of that."

"You just have to be able to keep up with me," I said with a seductive wink.

"I think I can do that." He smiled and gave my ass a quick squeeze. "Dance with me?" he asked.

"There's no music."

"Oh, there's always music, my love…"

———

While I left that afternoon full of excitement and potential, my trip to Kristin's office knocked me ten steps backward.

"How are things at home? With Dylan, the website? He still has yet to express concern over it?" she'd asked. Admittedly, it'd been a while since I'd made it to a session, so she was a little behind in the saga of my life. But the question had uncovered what I considered to be the last scoop of dirt she'd throw in my face.

"Actually, I shut it all down. The website. Dylan and I want to start a family, and it's just not practical for me anymore. Of course, there's this whole other pregnancy porn trope I guess I could pursue, but—"

"Oh, my. Wow, this is…unexpected, to say the least!" she beamed, cutting me off. She'd looked at me with what I could only assume was pride, her eyes lighting up in my presence for the first time. "I have to say, Alisha, I am *utterly* impressed." She made a check mark of sorts on her notepad, clicking the pen a few times before dropping it onto the page.

But I was nothing more than a deer in headlights, just waiting for the semi-truck to slam into me. Her sudden change in demeanor caught me off guard. "I'm sorry, you're impressed with what, exactly?"

"With *you*! Surely, you can understand how unprecedented this is. Your progress is remarkable."

"...I'm still not following."

She adjusted her glasses, and crossed her legs, tucking one behind the other like a proper lady. "You've come from virtually nothing, making a name for yourself in a lucrative and competitive industry. You built an empire of financial stability, and now you're in what I would consider your first monogamous relationship. And you're finally willing to give up your career to start a family." She paused for effect, and I imagined the perplexed look on my face alerted her to my continued state of confusion. "Don't you see?" she continued. "You're nothing like her—your mother. And, I know I shouldn't make that assumption without ever meeting her, but what I see in you, Alisha, is compassion. I see heart, and the will to not only love yourself, but to *be* loved in return."

She sat back in her pretentious chair, crossing her arms over her chest and smiling like the fucking idiot that she is. Of all the derogatory remarks she made over the years, I think that one stung the most.

"Yeah? Well, all I hear is your long-awaited approval, not *because* of all I've overcome, but rather a direct result of my decision to leave the porn industry."

She sucked in a breath and waved a corrective hand in the air, not having realized her mistake until it was too late. "No, no, that's not what I said. I just meant—"

"You didn't have to. Trust me, it was implied." I stood and threw my purse over my shoulder, the sudden tension in the back of my neck sure to develop into a headache later. "Ya know, at the end of the day, I'm still a sex addict. I still like to fuck and *be* fucked. And I'm not ashamed of that—

despite your attempts to convince me I should be. I mean, you told me yourself that I'd never be able to escape the title, so why not wear it proudly? And seeing as I'm all *healed* now, I'll no longer be in need of your services."

At that, I stormed out of Kristin's office for the last time.

Seven years of her bullshit was more than enough for me.

THE KIND OF PERSON WHO ALWAYS
LOSES THEIR KEYS

Alisha

I WAS NEVER much for holiday shopping, but Christmas was fast approaching, and while I didn't have many people to buy for—just Mrs. Maylen, Dylan, and a little something for Chris—I wanted to make sure their gifts were meaningful. If it weren't for them, I'd have no one to shop for in the first place, and I'd never bought a gift for a significant other, so I was stressing over what to get for Dylan. To make matters worse, thanks to my mom, I was a horrible gift-giver by nature.

But I was determined to change that.

I'd scavenged the outlet mall for nearly two hours, and was annoyed at the sheer volume of people in my way at every turn, the long checkout lines, and the fact that I couldn't for the life of me figure out what the hell to get for Dylan. Finally admitting defeat and throwing in the towel, I headed back to my car, the vibration in my pocket alerting me to an incoming phone call as I stepped off the curb.

The words *Restricted Number* scrolled across the screen. I should have let the call go to voicemail, but curiosity got the best of me, and I answered it.

"Hello?"

"Lisha?"

"Who's this?" I asked tentatively. Nobody other than my subscribers—and Chris—called me Lisha. None of them had my number, and Chris's would've shown up on the caller ID. I froze in place, standing in the middle of the walkway, my eyes scanning the parking lot while my heart hammered in my chest.

I recognized the voice on the other end.

"It's Lila!"

Fuck.

"Lila, hi." I spun around to get a look behind me, certain she was near but unable to prove it. I felt her presence, as sure as day. The thought that she might be watching me sent a shiver up my spine.

"Did you get a new phone number?" she asked, clearly aware that I did.

"Yeah." *How did you manage to get it?* I wanted to ask.

"I miss you," she admitted with a longing in her voice. I wasn't sure what to say, so I listened to the sound of her breathing instead. After a moment she asked, "Do you miss me?"

"Listen, Lila, I'm not sure how you got this number, but I have no interest in seeing you. Please don't call again." I disconnected the call, annoyed that I would have to change my number again. There was no way she'd be able to resist using it again.

I wasn't sure what to make of the intrusion, but I knew I didn't like it. One should never mix business with pleasure, and Lila—despite her attempts to prove otherwise—was nothing more than a former business partner, a colleague of sorts.

And she was chaotic; the kind of person who always loses their keys or can never remember whether or not they unplugged the curling iron. I didn't do well with chaos. I didn't do well with clutter or dust or people who buy frivolously.

And Lila was all of those things; the kind of woman whose brain rattles whenever she turns her head.

Sliding into my car, I chided myself for judging her; I hadn't meant to be catty. But I'd told her before, and my patience was running thin.

We couldn't see each other anymore.

I'd met someone.

That's what I'd told her when I called her following my ten-day trial with Dylan. House calls were officially a thing of the past—and not just for her, but across the board. I was going back to live streams only, no more private sessions, no more in-person hookups. It wasn't like I was under contract with anyone; I wasn't tied down in any way.

And I certainly wasn't about to ruin a good thing.

I'd told Dylan the same. He was on board, and even accepting of the fact that I'd still work. "I'm just glad you won't be doing those private sessions anymore," was all he'd said the morning I told him. He'd poured a cup of coffee, gave me a kiss, and headed off to work. I hadn't given it another thought; in retrospect, I should have payed attention to the underlying subtext, the snicker in his response. The upturn of his lip.

He didn't want me to work anymore.

He just didn't have the balls to tell me.

MY DARLING, LISHA

Dylan

STANDING up to Alisha was never my strong suit. Not that I *couldn't*—I just wasn't *good* at it. Sometimes I left her to her vices. I wasn't afraid to admit she knew better than I did when it came down to it. But there were definitely times I felt the need to butt in. She never saw herself the way others did.

The way others saw her started to matter, though. I hated to be the bearer of bad news, but it really did. After Grandma passed, Chris and I were the only two people who gave a shit about Alisha.

That fact would concern any husband.

Nobody cared about her wellbeing, whether or not she had a roof over her head, food on the table. A loving and safe relationship. They didn't even want to know anything about her, and once they did, they immediately judged her by appearance alone. Or, by her profession, if they happened to know what she did for a living.

People are dicks, they always have been.

But for some reason this was a surprise to Alisha. She cared so little what people thought of her that she truly had no idea how much they hated her. We all want what we can't have, and when we meet someone who has *it*, we instinctively despise them. We inadvertently wish them misery.

We want them to suffer.

And then we watch from the sidelines as they do.

I tried to explain this to Alisha. But as you may have figured out, my wife is quite stubborn—she never listens.

The day the flowers came, I admit, I lost my patience with her. Not at first, though, not right away. No, the argument took a while to heat up. I tried dealing with the situation politely, giving Alisha the opportunity to do the right thing without being told.

Does that make me sound a bit controlling? Oh well. Had you been in my shoes, you may have handled things the same damn way I did. When you marry a woman like Alisha, sometimes the jealousy creeps up when you least expect it. One day it's there, the next it's gone.

But it never goes far.

And when another woman sends your wife two dozen long-stemmed red roses, you better fucking believe you'll have some suggestive questions.

"She's becoming a bit obsessed with you, don't you think?"

"It's not like that," she protested. I approached the topic with a subtle urgency, because that's how I had to approach all things with Alisha. By calmly implying she was in danger and strongly suggesting she allow me do something about it.

"It seems like it is, Alisha. This woman is sending flowers to our house. She shouldn't even know where you live. It's…

stalker-like." I plucked the card from the table and gave it a quick read.

To my darling, Lisha.

"She's just lonely," she said in flippant rebuttal. Almost like she felt sorry for this woman.

"She has a husband..." I reminded her.

"She does." She rearranged the flowers on the table and stood back to have a look at them. I couldn't tell what she was thinking, whether she liked the flowers or not. "They're separated, though." She turned and grabbed the card from my hands, placing it at the base of the bouquet. "Not *every* husband is as wonderful as you are, Dylan." She stroked my cheek with her hand, her fingers tracing the edge of my mouth before the pad of her thumb slid across my bottom lip.

And just like that, the spell had been cast.

Her seduction began.

I wrapped my arms around my wife, pulling her close and pressing my erection into her hip. Her body responded, her arousal evident in the depths of her eyes, the beat of her heart against mine. She rolled her tongue along her bottom lip and slid her hand into my jeans, taking me in her palm and stroking slowly, taunting me without breaking eye contact.

Hurriedly, I backed her up against the dining room wall, my hands gripping her thighs, and lifted her until her legs wrapped around me. I pulled her panties aside—the fact that she wore only my T-shirt giving me easy access—and slid into her with ease. I took advantage of that moment to just *be* inside her, claiming her with everything I had to offer.

Then her mouth met mine, her tongue begging for me.

So I fucked her until she came.

Then I fucked her again.

Because those flowers sitting on our kitchen table

reminded me that if I didn't keep my wife satisfied, someone else would.

The fight that ensued later that night knocked the wind out me. To be honest, it was our first major blowout. The one that changed the tides and ruptured the dam. The culprit?

A simple question, really.

I asked my wife how many people she'd slept with.

Curiosity had been eating at me since the day I met her, and I couldn't stop the inquisition from falling out of my mouth.

Talk about a mistake, a big whopping clusterfuck of a mistake on my part. Word to the wise: don't ever ask your wife how many people she's had sex with. If you're planning to ask that question, do it while you're dating, but don't expect an honest answer, even if you give one in return. Everybody lies about how many people they fucked before they met their spouse. But should you feel the need to ask such a question, definitely do it before you get married and the answer that casually flies out of their mouth breaks your fucking heart right in two.

And most importantly, don't do it after sex, when she's sore and tired from riding you like a damn bull.

"Why the hell would you ask me that?" she snapped, popping up from the bed and stripping the sheet from the mattress. She wrapped it around herself like a toga, tucking the corner at the top.

"I can't ask how many people you've slept with? Is the answer *that* terrible?"

"Yes, as a matter of fact, it is. But thank you. Truly. For

making me feel like a piece of shit just so you can take pride in being the final notch in the belt."

"That's not at all why I was asking. It was just a question."

"And why does it matter to you? Hmm? You're the one that's here now. I already gave up my fucking job for you. What more do you want?"

Her blaming me for shutting down the website was the kicker.

She'd said it was a mutual decision.

Apparently, that was only the case until she needed something to throw back in my face.

A WEAPON MADE OF PAPER

Dylan

IT WAS OFFICIAL—MY wife had a stalker. A full-on, stage-five clinger.

And a woman to boot.

First the edible arrangements, then flowers, and the never-ending phone calls. The so-called accidental run-ins would come next; it was only a matter of time before she showed up at the house looking for her. I hoped it wouldn't come to that, but then again, I kind of hoped it would.

I went from turned on to straight-up freaked out in a matter of minutes and wasn't sure what to make of any of it. My concern was Alisha's safety, of course, and I was committed to ripping apart anyone who jeopardized it—man or woman.

So many thoughts raced through my mind...the first? Was she hot? And yes, I'll admit that probably wasn't the best first thought to have on the matter, but it is what it is.

Sometimes a man can't help but think with his dick.

Anyway, my second thought was a general curiosity as to what this woman wanted—what her end game was. Was she in love with my wife? Did she want to hurt her? I wanted to know what kind of stalker we were dealing with.

I had a hard time asking Alisha any of these questions, so for the most part, I asked none of them. Not because I lacked a backbone and harbored some unexplainable fear of my wife, but to be honest, I wasn't sure I was ready to hear the back story.

And I wasn't in the mood for another argument.

I assumed this woman—Lila, apparently—was either a former customer of Alisha's or a former…girlfriend? Lover? It didn't matter. All I cared about was getting her the fuck out of our lives.

"At some point, you might want to consider a restraining order," I'd suggested. Alisha huffed and brought her hands to her hips. I knew she was pissed at me, but all I could think was how adorable she looked when she was mad. The way her nose crinkled up, her lips in a pout.

"It's too late for that, Dylan," she snapped back. "She won't quit. What good is a weapon made of paper?"

"I don't know, but we can't keep doing this, Alisha. She's *obsessed* with you. How are we going to bring a baby into this world with that woman popping up everywhere?"

"I don't know," she snapped again, this time with more of an edge to her tone. She threw her arms up in the air and sighed. "I don't *fucking* know."

"Hey, hey…babe, it's okay. Come here," I said, pulling her close. She rested her head against my chest, and I inhaled the scent of her hair as I rubbed her back.

"Stop smelling me."

"I can't help it." I nipped playfully at her ear, and she

giggled, despite her mood, the sound of her laughter somehow erasing the stress of the day. I wrapped my arms around her like a claw machine. "You're kinda cranky this morning," I teased, my hand sliding under her shirt to her stomach. It was still flat, but the pooch would come soon.

The baby would be the change we needed; it would fix everything.

"What's your point?" She pushed my hands from her shirt and picked a sweatshirt off the floor before pulling it over her head.

"No point. More of an observation, really."

"Well, your unsolicited observation is noted," she said, smiling in that cute way that made me want to jump her. My heart melted, and all I could do was pull her into my arms and plant kisses on the top of her head. Those moments of vulnerability were so few and far between with her. I took advantage of them when I could.

A crack formed in my heart the following afternoon when Alisha suffered a miscarriage. She was only a few weeks along, but the loss hit us just as hard.

ONE HELL OF A GIVER

Alisha

I HAD ARRIVED at the hotel exactly thirty minutes early, as instructed.

A small suitcase in tow, I stopped at the front desk and picked up the room key. He'd said there was a surprise waiting for me inside, and the familiar chills of anticipation quivered in my bones.

The bed was littered with rose petals—a cliche I could've done without—and a bottle of non-alcoholic champagne chilled on the bedside table. Next to it was a small gift box and a card.

With the blindfold in place, I laid on the bed naked but for a skimpy pair of edible, crotchless panties. Even before he arrived, it was a high like I'd never experienced. A sensory overload of sorts. Everything was heightened without my sight.

The draft of cold air on my nipples.

The sound of footsteps in the hall.

Then, a soft knock on the door. I sat up, propping myself on my elbows.

"Are you ready?" he asked. "Did you follow the instructions?"

"Yes."

"Good girl."

Only a minute passed before the removal of his coat, followed by his shoes. I heard the sounds, was able to picture the scene play out, down to the color of his suit. Then, the slap of his belt being pulled through its loops.

A zipper.

A shifting of weight on the mattress as he joined me, his leg brushing against mine. I shivered at the contact, my heart rate rapidly increasing.

His fingertips grazed my body, from my breasts and down my torso. And I anticipated their touch on my swollen folds, where I expected them next, but instead it was his mouth, and it was—oh, it was fucking beautiful. My body writhed at the motion of his tongue, and I fought the urge to cry out.

And at the height of it all, there was something missing. There was something I couldn't hear, couldn't feel. And I was fairly certain that was against the rules.

Lila.

Fully showered and satisfied some time later, I exited the bathroom in the suite and met Grant in the sitting room. His iPad on his lap, he wore nothing but a pair of boxer briefs, and my heart skipped a beat at the sight of him.

He looked up and smiled when I stood beside him, and I

couldn't help but smile back. The shit-eating grin on my face had been difficult to wipe off after what I'd just experienced.

And as much as I didn't want to ask, I found myself doing it anyway. "Where's Lila?" He shook his head, but I couldn't place the expression on his face. "Is she coming?"

"It's just us this weekend," he said with an even tone.

"What about the agreement?"

"I didn't sign anything. Did you?"

Aside from your marriage certificate...I wanted to say. "No," I said instead.

"Do you plan to tell her about our indiscretion?" I shook my head. "Good. Neither do I." He motioned for me to join him on the couch. And I'd like to say the thought of having Grant all to myself for the weekend didn't excite me.

But it did.

It excited me a whole hell of a lot.

I'd wanted nothing more than to get him alone since the first night I laid eyes on him. And now that I had?

I had to admit, Lila's husband was one hell of a giver.

ASSETS TO WORK

Dylan

So, the truth is, I'd seen Alisha coming out of the hotel that weekend. I didn't know *who* she was, but I knew I wanted to be close to her. I was attending a Realtors' conference at the same hotel, and aside from sitting in on all the seminars and panel discussions, I'd essentially spent the weekend jacking off in my room and drinking from the mini bar.

Like a goddamned teenage boy.

Except that I was a thirty-four-year-old man simply hung up on his ex. For the life of me, I couldn't seem to pull myself together long enough to do anything about it. I certainly wasn't ready for another relationship—don't even get me started on my list of grievances about dating—and meaningless hookups had never been my thing.

I checked out of the hotel by eight that morning, taking a seat in the lobby to scarf down a pistachio muffin and a mediocre cup of coffee before hitting the road.

But then, there she was—the most strikingly beautiful woman I've ever seen in my life. She towed a small suitcase behind her, her other hand stuffed in the pocket of a long coat as she made her way out the door. Her heels clicked on the floor when she walked by, and I watched—almost as if in slow motion—while the sight of her burned its way into my brain.

Then I saw him follow her out the door. I saw her stand on the tips of her toes, despite the height she'd gained from the heels, to kiss him goodbye.

And yet, days later, I still couldn't stop thinking about her, and that was becoming a problem, because the chances of ever seeing that woman again were sure to be one in a fucking million.

There was no chance the two of them had done anything in that hotel other than engage in an affair.

That's when I turned to the internet. In hopes of finding her? No. I wasn't a fucking idiot—I knew I had nothing to go by, nothing identifiable to use in the search field. I stared at it, the blinking cursor taunting me.

So I set out to find someone who *looked* like her. Call it a fantasy if you will; I'm not entirely proud. Next thing I knew, I was searching through porn sites with key words like "brunette bombshell." Not because I had any inkling that I'd find *her* there, that *she* was a porn star herself—no, that fact was far beyond my imagination.

But sure as shit, there she was.

This goddess of temptation, right there on my computer screen. *Lisha's Bedroom*, the name of the site that I bookmarked and couldn't get enough of—but just the streaming and prior content videos, though. There were no private sessions for me, no one-on-one time with her.

Not until I met her, anyway.

All this to say to you—to *beg* for your understanding—
that I had no idea this mystery woman was the same woman
my grandmother had taken in all those years ago. I had no
fucking clue of that fact when I knocked on her apartment
door for the first time a few months later and found her
standing there in that kimono robe.

But after that? After that I knew the only way to win this
woman over was to take that secret to my grave.

"So, when are you going to fill me in on the whole Lila back
story?" I asked Alisha one night after dinner. We were snuggled together in our underwear, watching some cooking show,
and the question just leaked right out of my mouth.

Like spilled milk through the cracks of a kitchen table.

Did I have intentions of asking such a stupid question?

Nope.

Still kinda wish I hadn't, but it was out, and it was too late
to put it back. So I did the only thing I could think to do,
which was to ask a follow up question before she even
answered the first. "What's the deal with her?"

She shrugged, and even from my position on the couch, it
was obvious she wasn't in the mood for a game of *Twenty
Questions*. "There's really nothing to tell," she said, her eyes
never leaving the TV. Her nonchalance didn't sit well with
me, though—I knew there was more to it. Something she
didn't want me to know.

To my shame, I asked no further questions, knowing full
well that I should have. Instead, I stood abruptly in outward
annoyance. Her lack of interest in the discussion pissed
me off.

But, as she often did, Alisha put her assets to work.

We'd been arguing a lot lately, and neither of us wanted to go another round. To my surprise, Alisha slid off the couch and onto the floor, dropping to her knees in front of me, where she pulled out my cock and took me in her mouth.

The act was effective in shutting me up—and very clearly let me know that the conversation was over.

We never did get a chance to revisit the issue.

REJECTION REALLY IS A BITCH

Alisha

I SPOTTED her as I left the candle store, her blonde hair peeking out under a red beanie. Her disguise was subtle, but still enough for me to do a double-take.

She either frequented the same places as me, or she was following me again.

My money was on the latter.

I felt her presence, her footsteps behind me. I ducked into a coffee shop and walked straight to the ladies' room, locking the door behind me and pulling out my smart phone. Why? I'm not entirely sure, but I felt threatened, so I did.

I fired off a text to Dylan. **HELP. COFFEE SHOP. NOW.** He'd know which one.

The heavy door creaked melodically when she pushed it open, the lock turning a second later. The click of her heels, the stilettos she always wore, seemed to echo in unison with my heartbeat.

I silently sucked in a breath, sure to pass out as I held it in for fear that I'd make a sound.

"Lisha?"

Oh, God.

My heart pounded so hard in my chest, I was certain she could hear it thumping. That the very thing to ruin me would be the one thing meant to keep me alive.

She's looking under the stall doors.

She knew I was in there, despite my lack of response. Despite the fact that I hovered over the toilet, my ass planted on the tank cover. I fully anticipated her busting through the stall door, ready to assault the shit out of me, but to my surprise, she turned and left.

I hunkered down in that awkward position for a good half hour, hopeful Lila would have left the coffee shop entirely by the time I re-emerged. No one waits around in public that long when they're stalking someone, right?

Wrong.

Her eyes were the first I locked in on when I eventually stepped out of the bathroom. My legs went numb at the sight of her. She was perched on a stool at the coffee bar, patiently waiting for me and sipping an espresso.

She had ordered one for me, too.

"There you are," she said calmly, tauntingly. "You were in there a while. Tummy issues?" she asked, placing her hand on her stomach. She refused to accept the idea that I was hiding from her on purpose.

I nodded, almost grateful for the out but careful not to appear as terrified as I was. A woman like her thrived on fear. "Something like that," I managed to say.

"I saved you a seat."

She pulled her designer bag off the stool next to her and placed it on the counter. I stood in awe for a moment, quickly realizing I had no choice but to sit with her, to join her for a cup of coffee that—now that I think about it—she very well could have drugged or poisoned.

That kind of stuff didn't happen in real life, did it?

"You haven't been taking my calls," she said quietly, looking down at her cup. I avoided her eyes when she finally looked up. The sadness in them couldn't be real. It wasn't warranted.

"I've been busy."

"We're all *busy*, Lisha." She waved her hand in the air as she spoke, and I'm nearly certain I saw her eyes roll. I wasn't sure how to respond, so I didn't.

She waited a few awkward minutes, letting me sweat it out, and then reached over and took my hand. I fought the urge to pull it back, to break the skin-to-skin contact she had been so desperate to establish.

"Grant has been asking for you," she admits. "He—*we*—miss you." She paused for a beat, seemingly offering me a moment to take in her admission. "We'd like you to come back."

"Lila, I can't—" I started, but she cut me off before I could get in another word.

"Why not?" she snapped, her face oddly pain-stricken.

I sighed, allowing my growing frustration to overtake the fear that squirmed in my belly. *She's harmless,* I reminded myself. Lila was just a woman in love with the idea of opening her marriage to another woman. She was nothing more than a wife trying not to disappoint her husband.

I'd seen it more times than you might think, women forcing themselves into a ménage à trois to keep their husbands happy.

It rarely does, and most often results in divorce. Especially when neither party follows the agreed upon rules.

"Look, it's not your fault," I started, taking my hand back. "It's nothing against *you* or even Grant," I continued. "But I'm with someone now. I've gotten out of—" I paused, unsure how to phrase the statement. "*That* lifestyle."

I saw the tears well up in her eyes before the first one rolled down her freckled cheek. She was hurt. I couldn't blame her; rejection really *is* a bitch.

But you can't force someone to love you, and if you think you can, in the end it's not really love anyway. I reached up to wipe the tear from her cheek, but she swatted my hand away and abruptly stood from her chair.

"You can't just toy with people's emotions like that, Lisha. It's not fair to us." She spat the words like they tasted sour and scooped her bag off the chair. She didn't bother to wipe her tears as they fell. She had no qualms about crying in public, about making a scene over a lover's quarrel.

She was weak like that.

"Lila, come on," I argued, pulling a twenty from my wallet and tossing it on the counter. I had no idea if she'd already paid for our coffees, but I wasn't one to make a scene in public and leave without some form of condolence, so the barista was welcome to keep the change for a tip.

I followed Lila outside, running into Dylan just as I stepped out the door.

"Babe? Is everything okay?" he asked, pulling me into his arms. I could do nothing but watch the back of Lila's head as she stomped briskly down the sidewalk. At the end of the street, she turned and looked back, her eyes locking with mine as Dylan held me close.

How quickly the look in her eyes had changed from love to hate.

LIKE A DYING CAT IN HEAT

Alisha

ONE WORD RINGS in my ear.

Over and over, on a loop it plays. Like none of the other words in the dictionary matter anymore.

Murder.

Why it's there, I don't know. But it's there. It's loud, it's boldly written in all caps and highlighted in yellow.

And I fucking hate it.

I even caught myself humming a makeshift tune for it, as if an entire song could be derived of this one stupid word. But there it is, swimming in my head like that annoying jingle from the National American University commercial.

And I've always been a terrible singer.

Dylan used to say my singing voice sounded like a dying cat in heat. I wasn't sure what that sounded like, but figured it couldn't be good.

"The fuck you hummin' over there, Barbie?" Ronnie asks,

looking up from her lunch tray. She's been getting into some trouble lately and hanging around Tiffany a lot. I'm not sure how she ended up at my table, but she's here now, so I have to answer her.

"Hm?"

"You're humming something. I don't recognize the song."

"It's nothing," I say in attempt to wave her off. It'd be nice if she went back to opening her mouth only to stuff her face. But I seem to be down on my luck today.

She pitches a face and curls her lip in a half-cocked smile. "Ohhh, damn, girl. You...you wrote it, didn't you?" She makes air quotes as she speaks then laughs, throwing her head back like the idea of me writing a song is a stand-up-worthy joke.

"Not exactly," I say.

"Oh, cut the shit," she snaps, pointing a threatening finger in my direction. "You're losing it." She pokes at her temple with the same finger and stands, lifting her tray from the table. "Happens to the best of us."

I watch her leave, chuckling to herself as she dumps the remains of her lunch into the garbage bin. She hums my tune while she wanders off, waving her hands in the air like a dedicated choir director.

"I'm not the one losing it," I mumble to myself.

"Don't let her get to you," Tiffany says with a wink. I didn't see her sit down, so I don't know how much of the conversation she overheard, but I'm guessing all of it.

She's sneaky like that.

"I'm not," I say in defense, my tone flat. I stand and gather my garbage, deciding it's time to head back to my cell, but Tiffany grabs my forearm, anchoring me in place as she leans in close.

"I saved you a seat, you know."

"Where?"

"Over there." She points to a small table across the room, the loner table I used to sit at when I first arrived here. Most days no one sits there.

"Okay..."

"Next time, join me. It'll be good for your sanity in the long run."

And I don't know why I say it out loud, why I can't just keep the thought to myself. But the words are out of my mouth before I can stop them. "I don't know about that."

She digs her fingernails into my arm this time, a devilish look playing in her eyes. "Hey, ya know, I've been nothin' but nice to you since you got here, Thompson. The least you can do is acknowledge me when I'm in the room. I'm the only fucking friend you got."

And this is why women don't do well in prison, why emotions run hot. We're too needy, too high strung and territorial. It's like everyone's periods sync up and it's all we can do not to drown in the cesspool.

"Sorry," I mumble in response to Tiffany. She releases her grip on my arm, her fingernails leaving tiny crescent moons behind.

She stands and awkwardly leans in to kiss my cheek. I flinch when she reaches out and taps my crotch before she palms it and accosts me with her finger. "Just remember, there's no room for pretty people here. Prison makes everyone ugly. It levels the playing field," she says before walking away.

And the ugliest ones are always guarding the net.

CHANNELING OUR INNER DEXTER

Alisha

TIME STANDS STILL IN HERE.

Like I'm suspended in life, just waiting around until I'm allowed to go outside and play again. The day-to-day I once knew continues to fade away, the comfort of my simple life nearly long gone. I sleep. I eat. I shower. I piss and shit. I masturbate. Sometimes I meet with Kyle. And occasionally someone sexually harasses me. That's it, the daily cycle guaranteed to repeat again tomorrow.

Sometimes it feels like I'm drowning in the silence. I've been alone most of my life, but it's nothing compared to this. Childhood was a cake walk next to what I'm facing here.

I've never felt so unnecessary.

I don't know how to matter in here.

Maybe I never will.

During rec, I make my way to an empty table and sit down with a book. I've read it before, but I'll read it again just to keep busy. There isn't much to choose from here, and certainly no new releases.

But minding my own business keeps the other inmates at bay. Most days, anyway.

Lately it feels like they're all ready to eat me alive, though. Officer Marshall sure likes to take a bite every now and then. And that's part of the problem—he favors me, and they know it. They're never top choice anymore, and they can't take it. They need the dick, and Officer Marshall seems to be the only one willing to give it to any of us.

Not that I've resorted to asking for it.

My heart remains with Dylan, and I can't bring myself to engage in sexual activity with anyone here. Not willingly anyway. I *could.*

But I won't.

I can't focus on the words on the page. They blur together and my mind drifts again, back down Memory Lane, where it often likes to sneak off.

And then I'm with him again, with Dylan. Back at Mrs. Maylen's house right after it became mine. I remember the way his eyes sparkled when he laughed. How his lip twitched when he was aroused. Everyone has those little endearing quirks, and sometimes it's all I can focus on when I think of him.

I was a sucker for his lips, always had been.

"Dylan? I'm home!" I'd shouted as I walked through the door. I'd just dropped Chris off at the airport, sending him on a flight to Wesley Chapel, Florida, to the man he hoped would turn out to be his soul mate. I wished him well in his online dating adventures, but internally, I already missed my friend.

I was kinda pissed he left.

"In here!" Dylan called from upstairs. I took the stairs two at a time, anxious to see what he was up to, and why the house smelled like paint.

"Whoa, what's going on in here?" I asked. The expanse of our bedroom was covered from floor to ceiling in clear plastic. I mock searched for blood splatter, but found none. "Are we channeling our inner *Dexter*?"

"We're painting!" he confirmed, his mouth stretched into a wide grin. "Surprise! I thought we could get started on some projects since you're not working anymore. I know you're getting bored. Do you like the color?" I nodded and smiled at my husband's thoughtfulness, at his willingness to put my needs before his.

He knew I would struggle to occupy myself without working, to find a new hobby of sorts so that I didn't sit around masturbating all day. And Dylan's suggestion was to inundate myself with projects around the house.

"Come here," Dylan said, setting the paint roller in a tray and stepping over it. I held my arms out to him, suddenly wanting nothing more than to roll around naked with him in the wet paint.

"Hi," I whispered against his mouth.

"Hi back." His hand found my own, his fingers mindlessly twirling the diamond band on my left ring finger. "Feel like painting a picture?" he asked.

"Mm, I do," I replied with a hint of seduction. I pushed to the tips of my toes and met his lips, his hands already tugging at the hem of my shirt.

We were naked within seconds, our bodies molded together as I rode him in the middle of the floor, covered in gray paint, plastic wrap crinkling beneath us.

. . .

It's memories like this that make it hard to move forward here. Sometimes I forget he's gone, though, and that helps. That makes it easier to get through the day.

I'm not sure I have anything to look forward to otherwise.

BE THE TEQUILA

Alisha

THERE'S an old saying my mother used to repeat that drove me crazy for years—I didn't understand what it meant. I was thirteen, and far too young to properly place the reference, but for some reason I liked the way it sounded when she said it. Like she knew it was the most clever thing to ever come out of her mouth.

Maybe it was, who knows? I'd never admit it to her, but I kind of thought so, too. And, for some reason, it felt like motherly advice in a way, as odd as it sounds. As if there were a rare validity to her words.

While I made a point not to spend much time at home, I found myself stuck in the trailer over the holidays. Most nights I did my homework at Mrs. Maylen's with Teddy snuggled up to my side, his head on my lap as I studied. But over winter break my freshman year, Mrs. Maylen left for a week to visit her daughter and grandkids. Teddy went too. I had my own key to her house, but it didn't feel right staying there while she was out of town, so I didn't.

And a week at the trailer with Mom wasn't something to look forward to. Not only did she have nothing planned for us, there was also no Christmas tree, and no gifts to put under it if we had one—not that Christmas was about the gifts. I would've been content with just about anything, but what I wanted most was a normal day with my mom. The way things were before she found the bottle. I wasn't sure what everyone else's Christmases looked like, but mine were just like any other day, the only difference was that I didn't have school.

On the morning of Christmas Eve, I woke up to a quiet trailer, and sat at our kitchen table eating scrambled eggs and hand writing a research paper for history class. Mom had been decent company the night before, but it was a new day, and I never went into those expecting much.

She came out of her room around nine that morning, wearing a tattered bathrobe, a pair of crew socks that had seen better days crooked on her feet. "What'cha working on there?" she asked, her voice gruff from sleep.

"History paper."

"On what?" She grabbed a packet of instant coffee from the cupboard—probably stolen from the run-down motel she sometimes worked at—pouring it into a mug and adding water before placing it in the microwave. She stabbed at the buttons with a bony finger.

"The Great Depression."

"Ugh, story of my life," she joked, chuckling to herself. "I don't know why you're wasting your time with that shit anyway. It ain't like it'll get ya into college. Lord knows I won't be paying for it."

"I plan to go to college," I said with conviction. I didn't

care that she didn't believe me, I believed in myself enough for the both of us. I had a chance at a scholarship *somewhere*. It didn't matter where, as long as it got me out of there.

"The fuck you wanna do that for?"

"So I don't have to live like *this* for the rest of my life…"

"Ain't no such thing as a good life, comin' up like this, child. You were fucked from the moment you came outta me. Nothin' to do about it now."

Her words stung, and I wasn't sure why I let them. I tried not to value her opinion, but for some reason I did. I needed her approval more than I cared to admit.

The microwave beeped, and she pulled out the coffee mug and took a sip, her face souring at the taste. I wondered if she had any idea what a good cup of coffee tastes like.

"The cycle has to end somewhere, Mom," I mumbled, turning back to my assignment.

"For God's sake, Alisha, be the tequila, not the lime. Stop chasing a dream that ain't worth chasing."

Mom's words rang in my ears for hours that day. I may not have understood their connotation then, but I knew they held weight I wasn't ready to carry.

When I finally did graduate from college, she wasn't around for me to rub it in her face.

It took meeting Dylan for me to see just how wrong my mother was, and after that, I wished I hadn't spent my entire childhood—and let's face it, years of my young adult life—believing half of the convoluted bullshit that came out of her mouth. Sure, I took everything my mother said with a grain of salt, well aware that most of it was nonsense. But I was never entirely sure where the needle landed on the bullshit meter.

I had digested her insults into my heart and soul.

And they lived inside me like a demon, like a devil sitting on my shoulder.

Solitude is a strange thing. If you're anything like me, you don't mind being alone. You can live with yourself without going crazy. The quiet is cathartic, peaceful. It gives us time to reset.

But our minds like to play tricks on us, too.

Sometimes there are voices. Other times a general feeling that someone else—some*thing*—is in the room with you. You may even talk to them, have full-on conversations. And that's when you know you're going fucking crazy.

When the solitude starts to feel like a best friend.

I have nothing to do but sit alone with my thoughts, and my mother has been on my mind often. She had me convinced at a young age that I was unlovable, Mrs. Maylen was the first to suggest otherwise. She'd never came out and said it until the end, but I'll never forget when she did. I cherish those words, the truth behind them.

"Gretta?"

"Yes, dear?"

"Do you ever wonder what would have happened to me if you hadn't take me in?"

"All the time."

"Do you think I would've been stuck in that trailer forever?"

"No, not you, sweet girl. You were always meant for bigger things." I smile at the thought that she never failed to see something in me. That she didn't think of me as the burden my mother told me I was.

We sat in silence playing a hand of Rummy 500—she won, like always, her mind still sharp enough to kick my ass in any card game. I picked up the cards and shuffled them in case she wanted to go for another round. But her hand covered my own, and I set the cards off to the side of the table.

Instead, she held my hand, squeezing as if with all her might. Like the thought of letting go meant she'd have to say goodbye. "I love you like a daughter, dear. I hope you know that," she said before closing her eyes.

And I couldn't move. I held her hand, and sat there by her side, unable to do anything more than stare at the deck of cards on the table.

We were still holding hands when she drifted off to sleep, and it was Dylan who finally pulled me away from her a few hours later, when he came to pick me up.

It never was quite the same after she passed.

SO MANY DAMN QUESTIONS

Alisha

"FORMER SEX WORKER, Alisha Renee Thompson, has been charged today in connection with her husband's brutal murder. Sources say the wife of Dylan Thompson, a freelance Realtor, has lawyered up. She'll face Judge Wyman for arraignment on Thursday. More on this developing story on Channel 5 News at 5:00."

It happened quickly.

My arrest.

I was confused at first, my mind racing as the cruiser headed down the street. I watched my house disappear from sight. The home that I'd known for so long, now forever tainted, its memory tarnished.

At the station, the arresting officer escorted me to an exam room to be processed—searched and prodded for evidence, and photographed like the very crime scene they'd dragged me away from. They swabbed my hands, under my fingernails, the inside of my cheek. The cotton left a dry taste in my already sour mouth.

I could still taste the vomit.

I swallowed hard as the final swab was placed into a test tube, capped, and slid into an evidence bag. I wasn't sure what those swabs would say about me.

How much damage they'd eventually do.

"Hold out your hands," the technician instructed. He took my fingers one by one and clipped the nails, catching each of them in an evidence bag. I couldn't help but notice how ugly my hands looked. The absence of my long, manicured nails left my fingers naked. They looked like man hands.

Dylan had great hands.

The best hands.

I'd give anything to feel his touch.

After processing, I'm taken to an interview room and left alone, the lead investigator taking their time. I stare at my hands in a daze. They no longer looked like my own, not after what they'd done.

I stifled my surprise at the sight of a woman walking through the door, a no-nonsense look printed on her face. She took a seat across from me and slid a cup of coffee across the table.

I could tell it was burned without even tasting it.

"I'm Detective Adams," she said as she shuffled papers around in front of her. I wondered what was on them, considering we'd only just begun. How much could they possibly know this early into their investigation?

She looked up as if she was expecting a response to her introduction, but I wasn't sure what to say. "Mrs. Thompson, you understand why you're here, right?"

I nodded.

"Okay, well, considering the fact that you're about to be

hauled off to jail, I suggest you start talking." She sat back in the chair, suddenly looking smug, like she was putting on a one woman show of good cop, bad cop.

But still I said nothing. I was at a loss for words. Even if I wanted to share any, I couldn't. After a fifteen-minute stare down, she huffed and left the room, meeting her captain in the hall, neither of them bothering to speak in hushed tones. I heard every word as clear as day. Maybe I was meant to.

"The arresting officer said she isn't speaking."

"Make her speak then, Adams! I've got a dead body full of stab wounds, and I want answers. This should be an opened and closed case here, Detective. Open it...and then fucking close it."

The captain's footsteps echoed as he walked away, Detective Adams taking a minute to re-enter the room, probably trying not to lose her shit after being spoken down to that way. I cast my eyes downward, determined to avoid a too-close-for-comfort eye contact battle.

Cops love that shit.

Alleged suspects, however, do not.

And that's what I was to her. An alleged suspect.

"Mrs. Thompson, I need you tell me what happened."

I picked at a cuticle, the skin somehow still caked with dried blood.

Dylan's blood.

The detective sighed, her frustration increasingly more evident. I knew she didn't like me. She knew what I'd done—what I was accused of—and that's all that mattered to her.

"Mrs. Thompson," she began again. "We can do this all day."

I knew next to nothing about the law, but there was one thing I *was* sure of: I needed a lawyer.

"I'd like an attorney, please," I said. There was no tone,

no emotion in my request, just a stated fact. They were the first words I had spoken since arriving at the station, and while they were meant to protect me, apparently they were the wrong ones.

"Sure you would," Detective Adams grumbled, not even looking me in the eye as she rolled her own. She gathered her papers into a pile and stood, heading for the door.

Her mind was made up about me already; I didn't need to answer any of her questions.

It wouldn't do any good.

"I didn't do it," I said softly.

The door unlatched and she paused, holding it open and turning back to me. "That's what they all say." She exited the room, letting the door slam shut behind her.

I sat in that stale room for hours, waiting to be brought back to a holding cell. My mind raced as I thought of how I would've answered all her questions had I bothered to respond. But I was fucked no matter what I said.

What happened to your husband, Mrs. Thompson?

Did you have an argument? Catch him in an affair?

Did he put his hands on you? Maybe knock you around a bit?

Tell me about the knife. Why seventeen stab wounds? That's pretty excessive...a crime of passion...can you hear me, Mrs. Thompson?

Officer Jones finally returned at what I could only assume was an ungodly hour. He cuffed me, offering no leniency with the cuffs; they cut into my skin and tugged the hairs on my wrists.

"Let's go," he said, guiding me out of the room. He shoved me into a holding cell, and removed the cuffs again.

"What about my attorney?" I asked, well aware I should've been able to make a phone call.

"What about 'em?"

"I need to call one."

"So do it."

"There's no phone in here." He knew that, of course, and he chuckled to himself as he headed down the hall.

"You can call someone when I get back from lunch."

———

Kyle arrived later that afternoon. He didn't do much, other than ask a few questions and fill out paperwork.

"What happens now?" I asked, my curiosity growing with each passing minute.

"You'll face a judge for arraignment tomorrow."

"What does that mean?"

Kyle looked at me incredulously, offering no further explanation. I felt like an idiot for my lack of understanding of the legal system. As if I should've been familiar with the proper handling of a murder suspect.

"So, that's it? I just sit here?"

"Yep."

He gathered his papers and shoved a form and a pen in my direction. "For the retainer."

I grabbed the pen and signed my name as best as I could with my hands cuffed, the twenty-thousand-dollar retainer sure to be used up within the week.

"Don't talk to anyone in there," he reminded me. "Your case is already very high profile, and the media is in a shit storm right now trying to gather information. Say nothing."

Why the hell the media would give a shit about *me*, or why my case would be considered high profile, was beyond me, but I found out the answer to that question the following morning when an officer brought me something to eat, slipping me a newspaper in the process.

My face was on the front page.

Apparently, people have an interest in murder cases when the main suspect is a porn star.

I'm denied bond at my arraignment.

In addition to the nature and severity of my crime, the judge considered my financial means a flight risk. Kyle didn't even bother suggesting house arrest.

He looked anything but surprised when the judge advised I was to be transported to Smithson.

SLIM TO FUCKING NONE

Alisha

THE HECKLING STARTED ALMOST IMMEDIATELY. It didn't matter that I was sporting a bleak prison uniform, or that the makeup had been wiped off my face and my hair hadn't been washed in two days.

They all stared anyway.

Like vultures.

I pulled at the scratchy uniform, grateful, at least, that it wasn't orange, as Corrections Officer Marin led me to my cell. I tried to peek into the others as I walked past, but the preview did nothing to settle my nerves. It didn't matter what the cells looked like.

It was a cage, no matter how they decorated it.

I'm cat-called as we walk, my hands cuffed to my waist.

"Well, hot damn, look what the warden brought in for us today, ladies!"

"Did you see the ass on that one, Tiff?"

"Oh, shit, dibs on the new girl!"

A low whistle echoed in the space, and CO Marin chuckled at my expense as we approached the cell that would become my home for God-knows-however-long. "Looks like you already have some fans," she said, shoving a key in the lock. She twisted it, and the lock disengaged with a click, making me jump. "Step in, please." I did, and was instructed to turn and face her, to hold my arms out in front of me.

"Uniforms, toiletries, pillow, and blanket are in the cubby to your left. Head count at eight forty-five, lights out at nine." She unlocked the cuffs on my wrists and took a step back, on the other side of the yellow line that was painted on the floor.

I knew what it meant, what would happen next.

And it terrified me to my core.

She said nothing as she re-engaged the lock and carried on about her afternoon.

My hands trembled, and I pivoted to the toilet to vomit up my breakfast.

Kyle made an appearance two days later. He was my first visitor, and a small part of me was happy to see him. He was the only person with the potential to punch my ticket out of here, my one and only lifeline.

"How are you holding up?" he asked.

I nearly laughed at the question. At the notion that I'd give any answer other than, "Fucking peachy."

"Ah, what's eating you?"

"What's *eating* me? *THIS!*" I made a wide circle with my hands, motioning to the tiny ass room we were cramped into. "I'm in fucking prison."

Kyle rolled his eyes, compassion decidedly not one of his many endearing qualities.

"Beyond the fact that you're in prison against your will," he started, the sarcasm already heavy on this tongue, "you're okay, I assume? No one's physically hurting you? You're fed? Have a working shitter in your cell?"

"Fuck, Kyle, really? Is this how you treat all your clients?" He winked, avoiding the question entirely as he moved on to the next.

"Do you understand the charges against you, Mrs. Thompson?"

"Alisha."

"Fine, *Alisha*. Do you?"

"Yeah."

"Great, then you understand that this trial will be anything but a walk in the park. As I instructed the other day, you will speak to no one—not one single person in here, other than me —about your case. You confess to anyone, and it's over."

"Confess? Are you kidding me? I didn't kill my husband, Mr. Lanquist, and I sure as shit won't be caught dead talking to anyone in here."

"It's Kyle," he said, throwing my words back at me, and it takes everything in me not to crawl across the table and wrap my hands around his neck. "We have eighty-seven days to prepare for trial. That means you'll be seeing a lot of me, so I suggest you get comfortable. Don't expect any favors from me, and don't fucking lie to me. You lie to me, we lose the case, and you get to spend the next twenty-five years in this concrete palace. Got it?"

My posture deflated, the wind knocked out of me at the notion of spending what could very well be, the rest of my life in prison. And it hit me then, the realization settling in the pit of my stomach. "Oh, my God…"

"What?" he snapped.

"You already knew who I was."

"Excuse me?"

"You've seen my work. You knew who I was before you took on my case, didn't you?" The smirk on his face grew wider, his cheeks reddening just a bit.

"No comment," he answered evenly, and he's stoic as he crosses his arms, daring me to push the issue further. But I didn't. Kyle pressed on. "Sex sells, right?" he stated with a shrug. "Why else would you have benefited so greatly from your choice of profession?"

"My choice of profession is none of your damn business. My job is perfectly legal."

"It *was*, yes. But, for one, you no longer have a job, and two, a certain set of consequences come along with a career in porn—former or otherwise. Surely you know that by now?"

"What I do behind closed doors is nobody's business but mine."

"See, that's where you're wrong. *You* chose to put your life out there for the world to see—that's what your career did for you. Had you chosen a less public career, nobody out there would give a shit about you, and you'd be lucky to get a one-paragraph story on page ten of your local paper. But since you're a public figure, your life is *everyone's* business right now, Mrs. Thompson, and like it or not, everyone out there is completely infatuated with you. And not in the way you're used to, either. They want *you* to go down for this. They believe you killed your husband. And if you walk into that courtroom with a giant chip on your shoulder, your chances of proving even one of them wrong are slim to fucking none."

At the conclusion of his monologue, Kyle officially

became my one and only ally. For reasons unknown to me, all that managed to do is turn me on.

And that's an admission far more embarrassing than the invasive strip search I'd endured forty-eight hours prior.

"Hey, pretty lady, you lonely yet? Looking for some companionship?"

Ronnie.

The inmate in the cell two down from mine. I was sick of hearing her talk within the first few hours of arriving here. Sick of trying, and failing, to tune her out.

"Don't engage," CO Marin muttered, and I couldn't help but wonder if ignoring the peanut gallery did nothing more than put a target on my back. Still, I bit my tongue, my feet shuffling forward as we headed back to my cell. I didn't know my way around the prison yet, and while I wasn't sure my assumption was accurate—things had been a bit of a blur those first couple days—I thought I was on some kind of first-week probationary period or something.

I seemed to be the only one unable to move around freely, and always had a CO at my side.

"Don't ignore me when I'm talking to you, baby!" Ronnie continued, and I made the mistake of looking over at her. "I'm taking applications for my next in-house relationship. You gay for the stay, sweetheart? 'Cuz I can bump you to the top of the list if you ask nicely." She winked, and it sent a shiver down my spine.

I don't think she realized how little temptation her proposal held. Or, perhaps she did, and that explained the opening at the top of the list—maybe there wasn't even a list to begin with.

I looked away as CO Marin unlocked my cell, and that's when I heard him for the first time. I hadn't even been introduced to him yet, but the sound of his voice still made me cringe.

"Who do we have here?"

"Your newest inmate, Officer Marshall," she advised, rattling off my inmate number, name, and alleged charges. She'd memorized my rap sheet, almost as if to impress him, but I didn't hear any of it.

Because all I could focus on was the erection Officer Marshall was trying to conceal as she spoke.

TWELVE PEOPLE WHO GIVE A SHIT

Alisha

THE PROSECUTION IS SET to begin today in the trial of Alisha Thompson, the adult entertainer accused of murdering her husband, Dylan Thompson, a local Realtor. Channel 5 correspondent Lexy Dawson is live at the courthouse. Lexy?

Thank you, Cindy. I'm here at the Hennepin County Courthouse, where Judge Conwell Wyman, a twenty-two-year resident of the bench, will hear opening statements this morning, the trial expected to begin just after nine o'clock. I spoke with the District Attorney, John Hedland when he arrived, and he says the state is confident in their case against Mrs. Thompson. He expects a speedy trial, and anticipates justice will be served. We'll have more on this story after court concludes this afternoon. For now, I'm Lexy Dawson for Channel 5 Morning News.

I have no path to follow. No order of operations for the

remaining course of my life. I'm not sure what to make of that, but today I'm taking things one hour at a time.

I can get through one hour at a time, right?

While I hardly slept last night, I still managed to wake from a nightmare, dripping in sweat and nearly hyperventilating.

A darkness had flitted over Dylan's body.

He lay lifeless on the bed that we shared, the knife still in the shadowy stranger's hand. I tried to make sense of the figure but couldn't. When it turned, I gasped, the air stripped from my lungs.

It was my own face that I saw, as if looking in a mirror. It was my hand that harbored the murder weapon, my arm that drove it over and over, into my husband's chest.

As if the rage had taken over from the inside, desperately attempting to free itself from my soul.

I couldn't help but feel like I'd had the same dream once before.

———

"The media is going nuts. You wouldn't believe half the shit they're saying about you," Chris says over the phone. It's my last phone call before I'm transferred to the courthouse jail for trial, and his voice is the only one likely to calm my nerves.

I hadn't expected him to take my call.

"I don't give a shit what anyone thinks of me," I remind him.

He scoffs, his voice firm as he puts me in my place. "Well, it's time you start," he says. "Because those twelve seats in that courtroom are filled with the asses of people whose only job is to judge the living shit out of you. *You* are the only person who can win them over. Not me. Not your fancy-pants lawyer. *You.* That's your only job, Alisha. To give a shit about the twelve people who give a shit about you."

"Wow, Chris…I'm impressed. That was pretty good," I tease, while digesting his words.

He drains a sigh of relief, and chuckles a little. "Thanks, I am, too!" We laugh weakly before falling into a comfortable silence. It's been so long since I've heard his voice.

"So, only twelve, huh? No thirteenth person on that list?"

"Shut up, bitch, you know I love you."

And it's everything I need to hear. Chris's voice, his relentless ability to see the good in me, even when he shouldn't. As we hang up, I walk away with a smile on my face despite the charges I'm facing.

Because no matter what happens, at least I get to see his face in the courtroom.

———

"How are we feeling this morning, Mrs. Thompson?" Kyle asks as he enters the holding room. I already want to punch him, to deliver a heartfelt "fuck you" in the form of my fist to his pretentious face, but for now I appease him and settle for a snarky comment.

"How do *you* think I'm feeling today, Kyle?" He's not at all phased by my verbal assault—likely used to them by now —and I shouldn't be surprised, but I am. I hope this is a sign that Kyle can hold his own in the courtroom, but my faith in him wavers by the minute, so I let the thought go as soon as it comes.

"Any questions before we head in there?" he asks, digging in his briefcase. I take a step back and get a good look at him. Somehow he manages to look almost handsome in a dark gray suit and navy tie. He's usually more of a khakis and button down kind of guy.

I'm impressed, but don't admit as much to him. "No," I say.

He stares at me for a beat before an odd look settles in his eyes, like I've finally done something to please him but he doesn't quite know how to feel about it. I don't want to ask, so I raise my eyebrow and cross my arms over my chest.

"It's good, you looking like that," he finally says, waving a hand in my direction. "I like the subtle makeup, too. Makes you look more…" He trails off, apparently unable to settle on whatever insulting phrase is about to roll off his tongue.

"Don't bother finishing that sentence," I say. And even though I wish I didn't know what he meant by the comment, I do. Black slacks with a three-quarter sleeve blouse, a pair of boring flats, my hair wrapped in a low chignon and nothing but a layer of mascara on my lashes.

Quite unlike the pictures that have been in the newspapers and evening news. And oddly comfortable in comparison to my wardrobe as of late.

My image matters in the courtroom—just as it does in my prison cell and just as it did with *Lisha's Bedroom*. Each is a uniform representative of its own unique character, a persona enabling me to adapt to my surroundings for the purpose of survival.

The bailiff arrives and escorts Kyle and me to the court-room. We're seated at the defendant's table, and once my ass is parked in the chair, my handcuffs are removed.

I'm no longer sure what to do with my hands.

Kyle pulls out several folders before pouring water from a pitcher into a plastic cup, and handing it to me at the precise moment I realize I'm salivating and about to pass out.

I take the cup and chug the water as ladylike as possible,

already aware of the beady eyes boring into me from all angles of the room.

Within a few minutes, the prosecutor, John Hedland, arrives with his team of associates, each taking a seat at the state's table. I'll admit, they're as intimidating as they intend to be. I feel like a mouse playing a game of chicken with an elephant.

I don't find myself afraid of a man very often, but there's something about the way he looks at me that makes me want to crawl into a hole. His green eyes are piercing, but it's his stature that draws my attention. He has to be at least six-foot-seven—better suited for the NBA than the courtroom.

He and Kyle exchange greetings before Hedland turns to me, tipping his head in my direction as a means of hello because he's not allowed to shake my hand. He's looking at me funny, and I don't like it.

"All rise for the honorable Judge Conwell Wyman," booms the bailiff's voice through the courtroom. I stand along with the herd as the judge enters from his chambers.

Even *he* manages to intimidate me.

When we're allowed to sit again, Hedland smirks and glances in my direction, and it takes everything in me not to flick him off. If this is how the rest of the trial is going to go, I am most definitely fucked.

Just like old times.

HIGH FIVE, HEDLAND

Alisha

IT TURNS OUT, Hedland and Kyle have faced each other in the courtroom a total of six times.

Kyle has never won.

This fact would have been helpful three months ago when I hired him, but here we are.

As opening statements begin, I can't help but glance over at the jury, despite the fact that Kyle has instructed me not to. They are an interesting mix of jurors, almost like a modern-day *Breakfast Club*. I inadvertently make eye contact with two of them.

I don't tell Kyle about it.

For the most part, everything about the state's case turns out to be solid. If I were a member of the jury, I'd probably give Hedland a high five for taking another murderer off the streets.

Kristin's testimony kicks my ass.

As a witness for the prosecution, she provides expert testimony explaining, in great detail, the so-called signs and symptoms of sex addiction, the formal diagnosis she documented in my file at the demise of our one-sided relationship. Her professional opinion is even a matter of public record on account of the HIPAA authorization I erroneously signed at the start of our court-ordered therapy sessions.

Go fucking figure.

Her testimony is the first time the jury hears of my sexually deviant behavior—as Hedland likes to call it—but certainly not the last. The whispers and less than subtle glances my way were a clear indication that their judgment of me had officially begun.

Kristin is poised and confident as she answers the rapid-fire questions from Hedland, and later from Kyle. To be blunt, she fucking killed it.

Which is a shame.

She avoided my eyes while she spoke, and as much as I love a good stare down, I can't say I blame her. After all, I never did make a good therapy patient. Not only did she throw me under the bus with her expert testimony, she even managed to give Hedland the space he needed to run me right over with it.

To his credit, Hedland asked all the right questions.

Kyle, however, did not.

Cross examination does not go as well.

Dr. Lindsay—or Kristin, as I've always known her—is escorted from the witness stand. She keeps her head down as she passes by, and the realization that I have no ill will toward the woman lands right in my lap. I sure thought I did, but even though her testimony does nothing to help me, in the moment, I feel none.

She had been right about me all long; how could I possibly hold that against her?

Amongst others, Dylan's mother also testifies for the state. The show she puts on is equally as damaging, although she isn't on the stand more than ten minutes. After she's sworn in, Hedland is unable to ask any more than two questions. She's unstable, constantly dabbing her face with tissues as she sobs like a fucking baby on the witness stand.

And that's the only reason Hedland needed her.

To show the jury the poor, old, grieving mother of the deceased, and make sure she says the one thing that is sure to simultaneously break the hearts of all twelve of them: *"No mother should have to bury their son."*

Kyle instructs me not to look at her as she's escorted from the box.

But I look at her anyway. I watch her the whole time.

Because I can't help but think what a great actress she would've been.

POISON IVY

Alisha

"THE STATE CALLS Ivy Rogers to the stand," Hedland says, making a show of shuffling papers around on the table.

This is the final witness for the prosecution, and Hedland's last chance to prove the state's case, to convince this jury of my supposed peers that I'm guilty of murdering my husband.

And after that Kyle will try to earn his paycheck, although he gets to cash it either way.

A woman stands in the gallery, smoothing the pencil skirt that seems to hug her curves in all the right places. She's nervous, I can tell, but I doubt anyone else will notice. She saunters to the witness stand, her blonde locks draping down to the middle of her back. I can't help but salivate as I watch her, and my physical reaction takes me by surprise.

She's enticing in that girl-next-door kind of way. Like, the kind of woman who looks innocent enough for a man to take home to his parents, but once he gets her behind closed doors, all bets are off.

I've seen her type before; I've *been* with her type. And maybe I've been around women too much lately, because it isn't like me to pine over one, but for some reason, I can't stop staring at her ass as she takes the podium.

She turns and faces the courtroom to be sworn in, and my eyes instinctively fall to her neck. To the small mole just above her clavicle.

I've seen that mole before.

As if in slow motion, her ocean blue eyes settle on mine; they're vivid and startlingly intense as they bore into my soul with a desire only I can see. A seductive smile plays on her cherry red lips, and I suck in a deep breath at the realization that I know this woman.

It's her.

"Stop," I mumble, my body suddenly frozen in place, unable to move a muscle.

"What?" Kyle whisper-shouts, leaning in closer.

I raise my arm slowly and point to the witness on the stand with a shaky finger. "Stop," I say again. My mouth fills with sand, my knees weak, and suddenly I'm sinking, like I'm drowning in quick sand.

Judge Wyman bangs the gavel three times.

The echo reverberates in my ears.

"Control your client, Mr. Lanquist," the judge warns. Kyle tugs on my arm, which is hanging loosely at my side, a tingling sensation traveling through it and settling in my spine.

I can't take my eyes off her, and I swear she's glaring at me in the most provocative way.

Just like she used to.

She winks, and it's subtle, but I know I saw it. I hope someone else did too, because if not, I am truly, truly fucked.

I'm sweating and hot all over, and I let out a piercing scream before I drop to my knees. Kyle is at my side, his arms around me, trying to pull me back to my feet. The bailiff sprints over from his post, a hand on his service weapon.

The last thing I hear before the lights go out is Lila's voice.

"Tell me you love me," she pleads.

I met Ivy months before Dylan first knocked on my door, only her name wasn't Ivy.

And she wasn't blonde.

I'd met her through one of my regulars, Grant. His was a sugar daddy fetish, the need to provide for his woman financially, to watch her earn her monthly stipend through sexual favors.

It wasn't uncommon, but Grant was different than the others. He was sexy, and mysterious, and I couldn't help but look forward to our private sessions.

"Will you touch yourself for me?" he asks, a throatiness to his voice.

"Mmm, always." I bring my hand to my breast, pinching the nipple through the lacy lingerie; the skimpy fabric, that leaves little to the imagination, is one of his favorites. I make a mental note to thank Chris for picking it out.

"See what you do to me?" Grant groans, his strong hand wrapping around his cock as he strokes. *"I wish I could touch you."*

And he's said it before, how much he wants to have his way with me. They all say it, but when Grant says it, his words settle into my bones. I lean closer to the webcam to show him my cleavage as I press my breasts together the way he likes. He moans and it sings in my ear, the bass from his voice sending a tremor straight to my pussy.

"What would you like me to do for you?" I ask with puckered lips.

"Show me your tits," he says, swallowing hard.

"Oh, these?" I tease with a shimmy. I slide the straps of the garment down and slowly pull my arms through, my eyes never leaving the camera. My breasts tumble out, my nipples hard as the lace falls to the floor.

"You're so fucking sexy."

"Only for you."

"Mmm...show me."

"Show you?" I ask with a raspy voice.

"Yes."

"What do you want to see, baby?"

"Come join us," he says, and I raise a brow, the request unexpected. I didn't realize there was anyone there with him.

"Us?"

"My wife and I. We watch you together."

Oh, fuck.

"She's about to take my cock in her mouth," he admits, and I see her then, the back of her head as she slithers into view. "We want you to...ughh, yes, baby, just like that...we want you to join us."

My pussy soaked, I can't help but bring my hand to it as I watch her head bob up and down. "What would I do for you?" I ask, my mouth going dry.

"Play."

. . .

The following evening, I knock on the front door of Grant's luxury high-rise apartment, my pulse racing and a tingling sensation between my legs.

I can't believe I'm about to do this.

He answers the door in jeans, his toned chest on display, and I suck in a breath at the sight of him, at the divots in his hips. His dark hair is mussed, and I pick up the woodsy scent of his aftershave. His eyes trail my body, and he licks his lips. "Lisha," he says.

"Grant."

He steps back, pulling the door open further, and I walk in, my red Louboutin pumps clicking on the expensive tile.

"Take your coat off," he instructs, stopping abruptly in the foyer. I untie the belt and open the trench coat slowly; there's nothing underneath except the lingerie he sent me: a scalloped trim garter in white lace.

"Mm, good girl," he says approvingly.

He drapes my coat over the back of a chair before taking my hand and leading me down the hall. My heart is hammering against my chest, the anticipation intense, and I take a breath as we come to a stop at a closed door.

"She's ready for us," he says, and his fingers graze my chin, the contact sending a chill straight my nipples. I'm so turned on I can hardly keep from pouncing.

"Lila?" I ask, my voice gruff.

He nods, and pulls me to him, bringing his lips to mine. His bulge is prominent against my thigh, and I know this is against the rules we established earlier, but I can't stop myself from kissing him back.

We are not to fornicate independent of one another.

Grant pulls away without warning and turns the knob of the wooden door, pushing it open. It's dark in the room, but there's just enough candlelight that I can see her.

Lila.

She lies on the bed, naked but for a pair of black stilettos. She looks up as Grant and I enter the room, and brings a finger to her mouth, sucking it and biting her bottom lip.

She is stunningly beautiful.

Her dark hair is curled and loose around her face, her blue eyes coated with a layer of mascara and nothing more. And her lips...a dark shade of red that I know it will be all over my body by the end of the night. The thought drives me crazy.

She takes my breath away, and I don't know what to make of it. I've never been so attracted to a woman before.

Grant closes the door and comes up behind me as I walk slowly toward the bed. I feel his eyes on my backside, confident he likes what he sees.

Lila crawls to the edge of the bed, and I watch her breasts drag against the sheets, my own nipples hardening in response. She stands and walks toward me, and I can't help but admire the curves of her breasts, the sway in her hips as her heels click on the hardwood floor.

"Kiss her," Grant commands, and she does. She brings her lips to mine, her tongue dipping into my mouth, her hands already exploring my body. They're the softest lips I've ever felt.

"Yes, good girls," he says, unzipping his pants and stepping out of them. Lila's manicured fingernails trail down my stomach and make their way to the wetness between my legs. She finds my clit and rubs it gently before sliding two fingers inside me. I let out a groveling moan that she silences with her mouth, and all my senses are awakened, the heat of seduction sparking a fire between my legs.

I hadn't expected things to move so fast.

But I don't want to slow down either.

Grant takes Lila's hand, and they explore my body together. They touch, and knead, and caress in unison. He plants kisses on my back and along my shoulders while she kisses my breasts, and I'm in complete ecstasy as they worship me together.

They bring their lips together, me between them, and I lean into Grant, his cock hard and ready, brushing against my ass.

"Lila," he says in a throaty voice.

"Yes, baby?"

"I want you to pleasure Lisha while she services me. Can you do that for me, sweetheart?"

"Yes," she agrees, and her pupils dilate; she wants this as much as I do. I take Grant's cock in my hand and stroke it slowly. He moans, his breath hot on my neck. Without warning, he lifts me and lays me on the bed, spreading my legs and standing back to admire the view. Lila joins him at his side, and he gives her ass a slap before pulling her in and kissing her hard.

They stand at the end of the bed, watching me, the tension pulsing throughout the room.

"Isn't she beautiful?" Grant says to Lila, but she doesn't answer. Instead she climbs onto the bed and seductively crawls between my legs. He smacks her ass again, slapping his dick on it before burying his face in her. She squeals as a look of absolute pleasure spreads across her face.

I can't help but want what he's doing to her.

I tangle my fingers into her hair and shove her face between my legs. I need to feel her there, for her to taste me. She licks and sucks with greed, her fingers inside me as I buck my hips against her tongue.

And he's next to me in an instant, throbbing and ready for me, and I take the length of him in my mouth. He moans and squeezes my breasts, and I suck faster, my lips wrapped tightly around him.

Lila climbs on top of me while he fucks my mouth, and her breasts rub against mine. She kisses every inch of skin she can find, and I moan against Grant's cock. He pulls out and moves to the other side of the bed, stroking himself as he watches Lila make her way back down my body.

He enters her from behind, and she calls out when he takes a fist to her hair and pulls. I sit up, bringing my lips to hers, the sudden need to feel the smoothness of her lips again taking over. When she pulls away, she bites down on my shoulder before bringing her mouth to my ear.

Her breath is heavy as Grant pounds into her, her fingers reaching out and finding my clit again, and I feel the heat in my belly, the orgasm taking over everything in me.

She brings her fingers to her mouth, licking the taste of me from them, and I barely hear her when she speaks.

"Tell me you love me," she whispers.

And her eyes bore into my soul, the desperation in her voice lingering in my ears and swallowing me whole.

She sucks her bottom lip into her mouth and starts to cry as Grant fucks her harder...then she lays her head down on my chest, wrapping her arms around me like she's holding on for dear life.

ROLE PLAY, ROMANCE, & REVENGE

ONE HELL OF A HARD-ON

Dylan

I KNEW Ivy long before I ever met my wife. Did I realize at the time that Ivy was the same person obsessing over her? No. I never could have guessed, and I sure as shit didn't make the connection until much later, and by that time, it was too late. I had no idea she was the same psychopath narcissist who was stalking Alisha. And we've already established the fact that I overlooked a great deal after meeting my wife, so does it really surprise you that I missed all the signs?

I didn't think so.

Look, love can certainly be blinding. It fucks with your psyche. Makes you see shit that isn't there, and overlook the shit you *should* be concerned about.

And it makes you do some idiotic shit, too.

Like lie to your wife about your knowledge of her connection to your piece-of-shit stepbrother.

How was I supposed to know that Sawyer's wife—my ex-girlfriend—was the same psycho claiming to be in love with Alisha? All I knew of her was that she was an ex-lover of some kind—I knew Alisha had a habit of swinging in either direction, and I didn't have a problem with that. But I assumed this woman was a former friend, maybe an acquaintance of some kind.

Fuck if I cared to ask questions.

I just knew there was a woman.

And she had one hell of a hard-on for my wife.

And Lila? Where the hell did that name even come from? Ivy had turned into a fucking train wreck, like an accident on the side of the road that you can't peel your eyes away from no matter how badly it burns.

Ivy, once thought to be the love of my life—the first woman to poke a permanent hole in my heart—was now my stepbrother's estranged wife, and also happened to have fucked my wife, accidentally falling in love with her in the process.

Alisha had slept with *all three of us*.

This realization started the bleeding that would eventually kill me.

Because every man knows a broken heart never heals. It can be fixed temporarily, sure, but the holes will still be there when you look closely.

Ivy had always been beautiful: a petite blonde with the prettiest blue eyes I'd ever seen, a few freckles splattered across her nose. I thought she was the one. I thought we'd get married and have kids and run off into the sunset.

Then I caught her with my brother.

And six months after that, I met Alisha.

Ivy no longer mattered, and I hardly gave her another

thought. Had I known she was the same woman harassing my wife, I'd have done something to put a stop to it. Although, I'm not sure I would have realized her jealousy was directed at Alisha.

The common fucking denominator between us all.

EVEN COCKROACHES

Alisha

A MONTH INTO OUR RELATIONSHIP, and just a couple weeks before we were married, Dylan took me to meet his parents. Well, his mother and stepdad, to be more accurate. I had yet to meet his father, but we'd planned to take a trip out to Arizona after the wedding.

We never did.

Dylan told me to dress conservatively, so we stopped at the mall on the way, and I bought a pair of dark jeans and a loose-fitting sweater appropriate for an eighty-year-old. Dylan laughed at my expense, and despite the playful connotation, it pissed me off.

I'd done what he asked, pulling myself straight out of my comfort zone, and he couldn't even stifle his amusement.

We arrived at his mother and stepdad's Tudor-style home, with its well-maintained lawn and new cars in the driveway. It was obvious when we pulled into the driveway that they were the kind of people who flaunt their money instead of using it for good. I'd made a mental note to share a list of the charities I donated to each month—in hopes that they would consider doing the same—but I knew within minutes of meeting them that the gesture would not be well received.

"It'll be fine, babe, just be yourself," Dylan coached when we approached the door. I didn't bother reminding him that being myself was the one thing he'd asked me *not* to do, but I chalked it up as an inadvertent slight on his part.

His stepfather answered the door, pulling Dylan into an immediate hug while I stood behind them awkwardly. Bev stepped in from the kitchen, her privilege dominating the room like a fox in a chicken coop.

I wanted nothing more than to run, but my feet were planted to the floor. A fox could outrun a chicken any day of the week, even on Sundays when they met their future mother-in-law for the first time.

"We missed you at church this morning, son," she said in place of hello. Dylan nodded, neglecting to acknowledge her snide comment, and while he'd never admit it, I could see his disdain for his mother just as clearly as I felt toward mine. Their relationship was tainted just the same; they simply had different grievances eating at them.

"Mom, Jim, this is Alisha," Dylan said, placing a protective arm around my shoulders, as if he knew it were necessary. I willed my hands to stop shaking. My pits were wet with evidence of the nervous sweats I'd been suffering with all afternoon.

"It's great to meet you," I said, reaching out to shake Jim's hand, a mistake I hadn't thought twice about. I'd later learn secondhand that Bev found it disrespectful I didn't go for hers first. To this day, I'm not sure I did anything more than that to displease the woman.

"That woman is garbage, an utter embarrassment to our family," she'd said to the press. *"My son's good name has been dragged through the mud because of her."*

"Alisha, nice to finally meet you," Jim said as his wife's expression settled into a glare. It was obvious who wore the pants in that house.

"It's a shame your brother can't be here," she said, the jab landing as intended. I squeeze Dylan's hand to silence him, impressed when he managed to let it go without a word.

Little did I know the brother in question would turn out to be Grant.

Bev finally addressed me with a nod of the head when we sat down to eat, following what I can only refer to as a formal announcement of the dinner menu, a meal she had prepared entirely from scratch *as the Lord intended.*

"Alisha, may I ask what you do for work?" Jim asked.

Of all fucking questions, Jimbo.

I cleared my throat before dabbing at my mouth with a napkin, determined to pretend I had a semblance of table etiquette. "I run a streaming channel," was all I could think to say.

Dylan and I—in our haste to change my wardrobe—had neglected to discuss a backup career in the event that this very question came up in conversation. "What's a streaming channel?" Bev asked, her face turned up in confusion.

"It's just a website, Mom. Nothing exciting," Dylan chimed in. He placed a hand on my thigh; I'd said too much, gone against his wishes to keep my profession quiet. In my opinion, it was better to tell the truth from the start than to have it come out in the wash later.

But come out in the wash, it did.

Channel 5 loved nothing more than to air my dirty laundry.

My own father finally made an appearance after I ended up here; once my face was all over the news and in the papers. He even provided a copy of the paternity test to prove he was who he said he was.

Thirty years it took for the fucker to step forward.

And to my surprise, he'd known all along.

My mother knew damn well who he was—and so did he.

She was such a piece of work that my own father chose to make a run for it before she had a chance to ruin him, too.

Talk about a hit and run.

He has a family, my father. A wife, and two daughters in their twenties. Owns a construction company that's quite successful. I'm not sure what to make of any of it, what to do with this newfound information. All these years, he had the potential to save me from my mother.

And he chose not to.

His is the first letter I've received in prison, aside from the fan mail that never seems to cease.

I wish it had never come.

But even cockroaches find their way through the cracks sometimes.

GRAB A PEEK AT HER LADY BITS

Dylan

FOR ALISHA, the icing on the cake was when my father—not Jim, but my birth father, Weston—stumbled upon *Lisha's Bedroom.*

Look, it was an honest mistake, completely unintentional and an unfortunate happenstance. Did I have any idea that my dad watched porn?

No.

Should I have guessed?

Sure, probably.

But give me a break. I hardly ever saw the man. Was I supposed to bring it up casually in conversation? And who talks to their dad about porn, anyway? I highly doubt that's a topic for the dinner table, let alone a fireside chat.

And really, I should have known something was up when he called, practically whispering into the phone so his wife wouldn't hear him from the other room.

He'd made sure to mention that she didn't approve of his habit.

"It's not right, son. She's your wife, and everyone out there can grab a peek at her lady bits whenever they want."

"Dad, come on, that's not fair."

"What if it were your mother? Hmm? Think about it. A man cannot bring a child into the world with a woman like that. She's not mother material. Hell, she's barely even wife material. Trust me, that miscarriage was a good thing."

He'd said it so casually I almost didn't pick up on it.

I should have ended the call right then and there. I should have taken a stance against my father and put him in his place for disrespecting my wife like that. He had no right to speak ill of her, no right to judge her for the decisions she made long before we met.

And God knows my father made plenty mistakes of his own.

The fact that he was still, at his age, secretly streaming porn behind his wife's back was a prime example of one of those mistakes. I should have reminded him that every single one of those women was somebody's daughter. Somebody's wife, or mother. Who was he to think less of them for the very thing that made him so fond of them in the first place?

But what came out of my mouth instead was much worse than anything I *should* have said.

I didn't stand up for my wife.

I didn't tell my dad to fuck off.

Instead, I said, "I know, Dad."

Three words, morphed into a simple sentence with one comma and a period. That sentence caused more damage than the insult it was said in response to.

Because Alisha was standing right there in the doorway.

She'd heard the whole conversation.

THROWING EXPENSIVE SHOES

Alisha

I REMEMBER how she used to watch me, like she was in a trance, her eyes glossed over and slightly closed in that intense way that almost made her look high. I wish I had seen it then, all the signs.

Ivy is *Lila.*

The same Ivy who had an affair with—and subsequently married—my husband's stepbrother was *the* Lila who had been stalking me.

Grant is Sawyer.

My husband's stepbrother.

With this knowledge, I'm left in a constant state of confusion, my heart heavy and only growing angrier as the pieces slowly come together—at the understanding that everything I thought I knew was wrong.

That Dylan knew Grant. He knew Lila.

Lila and Grant weren't who they said they were.

And that possibility had never once crossed my mind, just as I had never suspected Dylan of his ill intentions.

But he had played me, too.

My perfect husband had kept a secret of his own.

He'd known all along who I was, had subscribed to my website, streamed my live events. Only, when he finally confessed, he didn't tell me the whole story—he told only the side of it he thought he *had* to tell.

The part he knew I'd already figured out.

But he left out the fact that he was well aware I'd fucked his stepbrother—that the first time he'd seen me was not the day he knocked on my apartment door, but rather at the hotel where I'd stayed with Grant.

And Grant? Well, he wasn't just a customer who had invited me to his room to play with him and his wife. He was a fraud, just as much as Ivy.

The Grant I thought I knew didn't even exist.

Sawyer did.

And *that* I didn't have the pleasure of finding out until after Ivy Rogers first took the stand.

Dylan made sure to leave that part out of his confession.

"I should have told you, I know. I'm so sorry, babe," he'd said the night he spilled the first intricate details of his deception, the night before his death. It was the cause of the argument our neighbors reported to police after his murder, the one that's been in the papers and all over the news.

There was yelling.

And shoving.

And throwing of expensive shoes like they were nothing. I had screamed, and cried, and demanded that he leave. But he didn't. Dylan never left during a fight.

Maybe this time he should have.

"I can't look at you right now," I said through gritted

SHANNON JUMP

teeth, my words like ice. He stood there, suddenly looking out of place in our living room, his face sullen and eyes puffy. They pleaded for forgiveness that would never come.

I had none to offer.

"Alisha, we have to talk about this. Don't shut me out."

"I have *nothing* to say to you!" I screamed, the words echoing in the expanse of our open-concept home. He stomped over from the kitchen, his face riddled with anger as if I were the one to have wronged *him*.

"Stop screaming at me!" he shouted, bringing his hands roughly to my shoulders and shaking me. "This doesn't change anything about the way I feel. Did I intend to fall in love with you? No, I *didn't,* but it happened, and I'm so fucking glad it did, baby. I love you with every part of my being." He pulled me to him and I shoved against him, pounding on his chest in hopes that he'd let go.

But I couldn't stop the tears by that point. The man who promised he'd never break my heart had singlehandedly managed to do just that.

My arms stopped moving, fists forming and resting against his chest, my voice barely above a whimper as I gave in and let him hold me. "You lied to me, Dylan...*this whole time.*"

He had won me over under false pretenses.

"I know...and I...I'm so, so fucking sorry. That's why I came clean, why I confessed."

"No!" I shoved myself away from him again, his words nothing but bullshit. "You confessed because you got caught!" His face fell at the legitimacy of my statement.

My husband had admitted to his betrayal, yes. Not because he wanted to, but because he had no other choice. He would have gotten away with it, too—had I not stumbled

208

across *Lisha's Bedroom* saved in his bookmarked links. The search history on his laptop had given him away.

The link had been saved to his computer months before we ever met.

Had I managed to piece together the rest—the fact that Grant was his brother—he may not have had to die.

So in a way, I guess that's on him.

NURTURING THE SEED

Alisha

LILA'S OBSESSION had blossomed like a flower in spring, one I unwittingly nurtured. I'd watered the seed and gave it room to grow into an unfathomable being of destruction.

And by that time, it was far too late to stop her.

I chew on the inside of my cheek, the nervous habit seemingly new and about as ineffective as all my other nervous habits. I pace the expanse of my cell and find myself counting my footsteps as my feet shuffle along the floor.

One.

Two

Three

Four.

But that look, it's stuck with me. There was something about it, as if Lila was trying to tell me something and I was too self-absorbed to pick up on it.

Her eyes.

Glossed over.

Squinted, the slits narrow.

Almost like she was in pain.

Like she'd been hurting for too long and just wanted it to end.

That's why, despite my lack of desire, I found myself out in bars with her at night. Grant worked long hours sometimes, and Lila's call would come through without fail, every Thursday and Friday evening. I don't know why I gave in and joined her; it wasn't like I used the opportunity to drink, but the atmosphere was nice.

And, for the most part, I didn't mind her company either.

I didn't feel as alone with her as I did around other people.

"Come home with me," Lila suggested one night after she'd had a few drinks. Her voice was low and seductive, like she thought she might be able to convince me with the same tone she often used on Grant.

"I can't tonight, I have a client in…" I checked the time on my phone. "One hour." She pouted and her eyes dropped to my cleavage, my breasts pushed together in a black halter top.

"I promise I'll be quick," she said, brushing my arm.

"Lila…"

Her face settled into a sour expression, her shoulders slumping. "You always have a client," she whined.

"Well, that must mean I'm good at my job."

"It doesn't have to be your job, you know."

"Well, I suck at everything else and have no desire to work in the world of corporate assholes. So, yes, it does have to be my job. I'm too young to retire."

"You could quit. Grant would take care of you."

I wasn't entirely sure what she meant by that, but I had no

desire to play house with Lila and her husband on a full-time basis. The sex was incredible, sure, and yes, I was openly enjoying extracurricular activities with each of them—without the other's knowledge—but no relationship needs a permanent third wheel, and I refused to be that person.

A third wheel isn't necessary when you know how to ride without it.

Not to mention, I wasn't looking to get caught in the crosshairs, and I intended to keep them both in a state of blissful unawareness about the amount of time I was spending with each of them.

I said nothing as Lila continued to stare me down, her face filled with dismay and disappointment.

"Whatever. I get it. Have fun," she finally said after an awkward minute. She stood and grabbed her clutch, tucking it under her arm. I couldn't help but roll my eyes; these kind of theatrics were one of the reasons I never cared to entertain female friends.

I watched Lila stomp out of the bar, never once turning back to see if I cared enough to watch her leave. I didn't, not really, but I couldn't help but watch her anyway. I wondered how Grant managed to put up with her.

Turning back, I raised a finger to flag down the bartender, realizing with annoyance that she hadn't paid her tab.

DON'T THANK ME YET

Alisha

I TELL KYLE EVERYTHING.

Everything I can think to tell him about Lila, about Grant. And for the first time since I met the prick, he actually looks like he feels sorry for me. Like he believes the words pouring out of my mouth like vomit—that I didn't kill my husband. That I've been set up.

He looks sick, his face ashen like he might pass out or, at the very least, barf all over the floor.

"I'm going to request a continuance," he says after a minute, as if a continuance will magically fix everything. It's no more helpful than applying a bandage to a bleeding wound after the bleeding has already stopped.

He's too late.

"What will that do?" I ask, willing my hands to stop shaking. I pick at the cuticles, at the dry skin that now covers my hands. I can't get the image of her out of my head, that hateful look that was in her eyes.

"It'll buy us some time," Kyle says. He runs his hands through what's left of his hair and breathes heavily.

"Time for what, exactly?"

"We need to investigate further. See what we can find out about Lila—or Ivy—whatever the fuck her name is. Her past. Look into her alibi. Our defense is built entirely on reasonable doubt, and now we finally have it." He avoids my eyes as he speaks, rattling off his to-do list while he scribbles it on a sheet of lined paper. His pen moves frantically, and I can't help but wonder what the hell happens next.

He can't save me.

"Kyle?"

He stops writing and looks at me with apologetic eyes. To my surprise, I place a hand over his. "Yeah?"

"Thank you." It's all I can think to say, these two tiny, insignificant words that mean nowhere near enough.

"Don't thank me yet," he says, suddenly popping up from his chair and leaving the room. I stare at the stale gray door, my mind suspended in time, remembering that first night I met Lila and wondering how the hell I never considered the fact that she and Grant would give me fake names.

Lila.

Ivy.

Grant.

Sawyer.

The pieces fit together like a lock and key.

How did I miss so much?

Dylan had known all along—he *knew* Ivy was dangerous. That she would ruin me. Ruin us. I was well aware that she was crazy, sure, but I never suspected she was capable of *this* —of murder. That she'd take my husband from me.

He tried to warn me.

I try to make sense of everything I've learned, of this new information that probably isn't all that new when I think about it hard enough.

Dylan was naked when I found him.

In our bed.

Traces of semen—Dylan's—were found in the blood specimens, which I'd learned in court during the prosecution's testimony, the shock probably written all over my face for the jury to see. For them to misinterpret along with all the other evidence against me.

Did she fuck my husband?

It's the only logical explanation. Dylan always slept in his boxers—said the sheets tickled his dick when he slept in the buff.

So, why was he naked?

He would never cheat on me, not Dylan. Never in a million years, especially with the very same woman who'd done it to him.

Right?

Kyle returns less than twenty minutes later, sweat slick across his forehead, his shirt partially untucked.

Judge Wyman has denied our request for continuance.

LIKE A MONSTER UNDER MY BED

Alisha

ALL THE AIR deflates from my lungs when Ivy is called back to the stand. She's sworn in as Kyle's pen slithers on the page in front of me, and I don't want to look at the words he's written, but I can't help it, so I do.

Calm down, he writes, underlining it with a final swipe of the pen.

But the words seem to have the opposite effect on me. Ivy's presence in the courtroom is too much. I want to crawl under the table and hide. She's like a monster under my bed, a demon I can't escape no matter how hard I try, not even in the dark.

Hedland approaches his witness. He smiles, and she smiles back, tight-lipped, so she doesn't show her teeth. She knows they're sharp and doesn't want the jury to see.

She's filled out since I last saw her. I hadn't noticed it the other day, but I do now. She looks different somehow, and it's not just because her hair is a different color. Maybe it's the fit of her skirt, the way it sits on her hips. Maybe it's the loneliness that's gotten to her.

I've never been as equally afraid of, and attracted to, a monster, but that's the pull I feel in my chest seeing her up there. I want to run full-on in the other direction, yet I can't fucking look away.

"Can you please state your name for the record?" Hedland asks.

"Ivy Rogers, sir."

"And your relationship to the defendant, Mrs. Rogers?" Her eyes reach mine, and it's all I can do not to blink. To hide behind the fear. She's nervous, despite the perversity behind her eyes. Like she wants to please me, or make me proud, even now.

"We're former lovers," she says, and a hush falls over the room—over the jury—and even Judge Wyman is outwardly taken aback by Ivy's confession.

It wasn't what I expected to hear either.

"Could you be more specific? Had you and Mrs. Thompson entered into a formal relationship?"

"Not exactly."

"Help us understand."

"Alisha—I mean, Mrs. Thompson—" she corrects herself, clearing the frog in her throat. "Was involved…sexually… with me and my husband."

"Your husband," Hedland starts, making a show of looking at the sheet of paper in his hand, even though he probably doesn't need it. "…is Sawyer Rogers. Is that correct?"

"Yes," she says, nodding. The jury doesn't pick up on the significance of it yet. They can't possibly know, because the last names are different. They're not related by blood.

It's one of the reasons I missed it, too.

"Tell me, Mrs. Rogers, is your husband here today?"

"No."

"And why not?"

"My husband and I are separated."

"Why is that?"

"Objection, speculation."

"Sustained."

"When did you and your husband separate?"

"About two months after Alisha ended our arrangement."

"And what exactly was your arrangement?"

"Sawyer and I invited Alisha into our bedroom under the agreement that she would engage—sexually—but only with *both* of us present."

"And did all parties stick to that arrangement?"

"No."

"Who strayed?"

"We all did," she admits, looking down at her lap. She's playing the jury, acting as if she's ashamed, but I know she's not. She was the first to stray.

"So, is it safe to say your marriage was jeopardized as a direct result of Mrs. Thompson's involvement? That perhaps she was the cause of your marital problems?"

"Objection again, Your Honor. This is ridiculous." Kyle says smoothly, gesturing at Hedland with a flippant hand.

"Overruled. You may answer the question, Mrs. Rogers."

"Yes."

"Tell me, were you aware of your husband's relation to Dylan Thompson, the deceased?" She freezes, the question seemingly startling her, as if Hedland had phrased it differently during trial preparations.

"I...yes, I was."

"And what was the relationship between Dylan Thompson and Sawyer Rogers?"

"They were stepbrothers."

———

The tone in the room has changed at Ivy's admission of Dylan and Sawyer's relation. I see the apprehension in the jury, in their newly stiffened body language. Their notebooks readily open on their laps. They see this turning point for what it is— a potential redirect of opinion.

Kyle approaches the witness stand with a swagger I haven't yet seen from him. He appears confident for cross examination, his eyes like daggers as they bore into Ivy's. He's rehearsed these questions so much that he doesn't even open his folder, just leaves it sitting on the table next to me. I shuffle in my seat, the nerves swimming in my belly.

"How did you come to know your husband, Mrs. Rogers?" he asks with an even tone.

"I met him through his brother, Dylan."

"And, if I understand correctly, you were involved in a long-term relationship with Mr. Thompson, and later with his stepbrother, Sawyer Rogers?"

She nods tentatively, swallowing slowly. She knows where Kyle is headed, and she doesn't like it.

"I need a yes or no, Mrs. Rogers."

"Yes."

"And did you end the relationship with Mr. Thompson prior to pursuing a relationship with his stepbrother?"

She glares suddenly, the break in her resolve palpable. "No."

"So, is it safe to say you're well-versed in the art of deception?"

"Objection!" Hedland bellows from the opposing table.

"Sustained."

"Rephrase, Your Honor. Mrs. Rogers, how long did you pursue a relationship with Sawyer Rogers behind his step-brother's, back?"

Ivy looks to Judge Wyman as if to ask if she's required to answer the question. Wyman nods and waves a hand, encouraging her to proceed. "Um…I'm not sure," she finally says.

"I'll wait, if you need a moment."

"I think it was about four months."

"Four months. That's an awful long time to engage in an affair."

"The court is not the place for opinions, Mr. Lanquist. Ask a question," Wyman says with annoyance.

"I'm sorry, really quick—can you remind the jury of your first name, Mrs. Rogers?"

"Objection, the witness has already stated her name for the record."

"Overruled."

Ivy squirms in her seat, beads of perspiration forming above her brow. She knows what's coming, and she doesn't like it, but it won't matter.

"Ivy."

"Hmph. That's odd, my client seemed to be under the impression you went by a different name. Lila, was it?"

She pauses, taking her time before replying through gritted teeth, "Yes."

Kyle waits for the jury to react. Several of them make note of the response, and anticipation knocks in my chest. I lace my fingers together, holding my own hands to prevent them from shaking.

"It was a safety precaution. My husband and I didn't feel comfortable sharing our real names."

"And how long were the two of you involved in a sexual relationship with my client?"

"A few months. Give or take."

"During that time, did you ever confess your real names to her?"

"No."

"Did you ever inform my client of your husband's familial relationship to Dylan Thompson?"

"No."

"Even though it seemed likely you might run into her outside of the nature of the relationship? Perhaps at family gatherings, holidays?"

"Correct."

"Why not?"

"Sawyer and Dylan hadn't spoken to one another in several years. We didn't attend family events where Dylan and Alisha were present."

"Why were Sawyer and Dylan not speaking?" I expect an objection from Hedland, but it never comes. He looks about as entranced as the jury. He's not even taking notes.

Ivy swallows hard, and I see the change in her eyes. The moment the fear changes to anger. She sees red, the fire in her eyes enough to burn a hole through Kyle's head.

"They hadn't been on speaking terms since Dylan discovered our affair."

"Ah. Okay, that makes sense. So, essentially, you tore the family apart, did you not?"

"Objection!"

There it is.

"Sustained. Mr. Lanquist, you're on thin ice with this line of questioning."

"My apologies, Your Honor." Kyle pauses, casually brushing a palm across his forehead. "Just one more sequence of questions here. Mrs. Rogers, at what point did you begin stalking my client?"

Hedland erupts, and all I can do is relax into my seat and fight like hell to suppress a smile. I'd give anything for a bowl of popcorn right now; this is turning into quite the show.

I can't help but commend Kyle for his resolve in the courtroom today. Never once did he mention that I'd met Ivy and Sawyer—*Lila and Grant*—because they were paying clients. And that was a good thing; any time we could help the jury forget what I did to earn a living was a point for the defense.

Apparently I'd given Kyle much less credit than he deserves.

He's even managed to steer the jury away from the notion that my profession was the cause of their separation, instead focusing on Ivy's expert ability to maintain her deception.

He was fucking brilliant in there.

Suddenly I find myself fighting the urge to drop to my knees and take Kyle's dick in my mouth. He deserves appreciation for his hard work today.

It seems Ivy Rogers has finally met her match.

SPELL IT OUT FOR THE JURY

Alisha

MUCH TO MY CHAGRIN, Chris is never called to the stand; Kyle has decided not to question him as a witness for the defense, even though I'm adamant we need him. I fight Kyle on this, on the fact that, without Chris, there is literally no one else to speak on my behalf.

We have no other witnesses.

And that's when Kyle decides to tell me that he's putting me on the stand.

The whispers from the gallery grow louder as I'm sworn in and take a seat in the box. My testimony under Kyle's line of questioning is smooth. There are no surprises.

It's short and sweet, like when I lost my virginity.

The true dance begins when Hedland stands, making a show of his presence in the center of the room, buttoning his suit jacket slowly while everyone else waits for him to start.

The first few questions aren't too bad.

But they grow increasingly more difficult—more damaging—as he goes on.

"Is it safe to say you've earned your living by seducing people?"

"Objection, Your Honor!" Kyle's voice booms from the table. He looks funny over there all by himself, different from this angle for some reason. He's objecting a lot, but Judge Wyman keeps shutting him down, and even when he doesn't, Hedland just finds new ways to ask different questions that result in the same damaging response as the original.

"Sustained."

"I'll reword. Mrs. Thompson, what do you do for work?"

I look to Kyle, his expression unreliable, but I read it anyway.

You're fucked.

But I can't break down now.

"I run a website—a content channel."

"What kind of content channel?"

"Not the kind that's kid-friendly," I admit, and at least one member of the jury scoffs at the response, a reminder that I need to reel in the sarcasm.

"What's the basis of the show?"

"Well, it's not a show, per se."

"What is it then?"

"A live stream."

"Of?"

I suck air into my lungs, ashamed of my career for the first time since its inception; Kristin's testimony was nothing compared to this. Hedland's about to put me in my place, and I'm not sure how to stop him. "Adult content," I finally say, certain it comes out more like a mumble.

"Adult content…as in porn?"

"Not exactly."

"Enlighten us, Mrs. Thompson. Spell it out for the jury." He smirks, and I want nothing more than to slap his lips off his face. I have no doubt that Hedland himself is well-educated on the meaning of adult content. Kyle objects but is overruled. Hedland turns to the judge, flippantly explaining the line of questioning.

"Your Honor, the defendant's profession is an intricate part of this case. It establishes not only her questionable character, but her compulsivity and perverse nature."

And this is where Kyle's lack of witness coaching gives Hedland an upper hand.

I push to my feet.

In the witness box.

Pointing a finger right in the prosecutor's smug face.

"So, you're implying that because I work in a *legal* sex industry, that I have no character? Is that what you're saying, Mr. Hedland?"

The bailiff approaches as I realize my mistake and sit back down.

"There will be no further outbursts from you, Mrs. Thompson. And you are to stay seated while you're on the stand, is that understood?"

"Yes," I say, slumping in the seat.

"Mr. Lanquist, you will advise your client to speak only when spoken to. The attorneys will ask the questions around here." Kyle shoots me a look, nodding to Judge Wyman in the process.

"The defense would like to request a short break, Your Honor," he says to my surprise. Wyman rolls his eyes and makes a show of checking the clock.

We're grateful when he allows the break.

In the holding room, Kyle kindly tears me a new asshole.

"You absolutely *cannot* react like that on the stand, Alisha. The jury will hang you in a heartbeat."

"What am I supposed to do, Kyle? Put on a nun's cloak, strap on the rosary, and say my fucking prayers?"

"That's funny," he says mockingly. "Stick to the script. We discussed this, remember? You can't lose your cool up there, not after all we've accomplished. That jury is unsure, I can see it in their eyes...and do you know what that means?"

"That we have a chance?" I say tentatively.

"That we have a chance," Kyle confirms with a nod.

TELL ME YOU LOVE ME

Alisha

"Has the jury reached a unanimous verdict?" Judge Wyman asks the jury foreperson. Her nerves are palpable throughout the room, and she clears her throat as she approaches a microphone. "We have, Your Honor."

There's a hush over the courtroom as the clerk asks for the reading of the verdict. I forget to breathe as it's read, the words seemingly spoken at a snail's pace, but no matter how fast or slow they come out, they're still the same in the end.

I fight the urge to scream, to kick and punch and throw myself onto the floor in a tantrum of epic proportions.

My body wants to protest when the bailiff approaches with handcuffs.

I hear nothing but the click of the locks as they slide into place. And it's as if the sound is nearly a thousand decibels louder than anything else in this room.

It may as well be a noose.

I've just been convicted of murder.

The courtroom doors open and the media are allowed back in, their cameras' red lights taunting me from all angles now. Everything suddenly seems too loud.

The shuffle of feet, a throat-clearing cough, the ticking of the clock.

Until everything eventually blurs together, and I can't move. As if I'm suspended, floating in the air above me, watching this scene play out like I'm the star of the movie.

Kyle's head falls into his hands—he knows he has failed. He's let me down.

I scan the room in search of Chris, of the last of the thirteen people who might still give a shit about me. But it's Bev that I see instead, and that hatred behind her eyes is devastating. The upturn of her lips that tells me she thinks I got what was coming to me, that she, too, is without a doubt that I murdered her son.

"This way, Mrs. Thompson," the bailiff says, and Kyle stands. Looking into his eyes is painful; I feel his remorse in my bones.

He should have done more.

He should have tried harder, believed me a little sooner.

We would have had more time.

"We'll appeal," he says with little confidence. I say nothing as I'm dragged away, back in the direction of the holding cell.

I see her then, just before the door closes, and I can't tell if she's happy or sad. She's just there. Present, but aloof, a single tear rolling down her cheek.

"Tell me you love me," she whispers.

THOMPSON, MURDER FOR ONE

Dylan

SHE SHOWED up out of nowhere, crawling into our bed as if she belonged there. As if I wanted her there. Half asleep, I didn't register that it was her. I knew Alisha had left for her morning run, but I thought she had come back early. That maybe she wasn't up for a run that morning after all.

But it wasn't Alisha.

It was a blonde woman, one I recognized, and for a moment I about shit myself when she grabbed hold of the duvet and yanked it off the bed and onto the floor. "What the fuck!" I yelled, realizing with a start that she'd cuffed my hands to the headboard as well.

"Don't be alarmed, Dylan. I'm just here to have a little conversation with you," she crooned, her lips shaping into a crooked smile.

I was about to ask what she was doing in my house, in my bed, but the sound of her voice made it clear: she had come for revenge. And it was finally clear who had been stalking my wife.

"Lila?"

"Oh, *good*, she did tell you about me!" she said, pleased with my answer.

Her hand trailed over my stomach and I shook it off, an edge to my tone as I said, "Of course she did. I just...didn't think it was you."

"Ah, and I bet you probably never mentioned how *you* know me either. Did you?"

I said nothing, unable to admit I'd been too cowardly to come forward with the whole story.

Ignoring her question, I writhed on the bed, attempting to wake the muscles in my forearms enough to crack the headboard and pry myself loose.

But Alisha and I had invested in a sturdy headboard right from the start—we'd tested its strength many times.

It wasn't going anywhere.

And these weren't those cheap fuzzy cuffs you'd buy at a sex store—they were the real deal, and it was at that point that I started to get a little worried.

But despite the fact that I was restrained against my will, I couldn't hide my apparent arousal. I willed my cock to shrivel up and go back into hiding, but Ivy was a beautiful woman. And she was taking her clothes off, folding them neatly and placing them in a duffle bag. My confused cock raised to a full stance, on high alert and ready to play.

She stripped naked.

Then she climbed onto my lap, rubbing her wetness on my leg as she positioned herself. My dick throbbed at the sight of her, and I knew I was screwed. The last thing I ever wanted to do was cheat on my wife, but I couldn't seem to get that memo to my stupid dick. Ivy leaned down and kissed the tip of it, and for some fucking reason I moaned.

That only turned her on more.

I tried the age-old trick of thinking of something else —*Grandma. Dog shit. Rotten milk. Vomit.* Nothing worked... and then her tongue...*oh fuck, I forgot how good she is at that.*

"It's your fault she left us, you know," she said, her lips coming off my cock as she looked up at me through sultry eyes. Her breath teased my dick as she spoke. "You took her from us, Dylan. The three of us could've been something."

"You deserved it," I mumbled through labored breaths. "For what you did to me..." Her tits brushed against my thighs, and as if it wasn't enough that she'd taken me in her mouth again, she brought a hand to her pussy.

And then she was on top of me, and I knew she was about to sit on my cock, and despite myself—despite everything I knew—in that moment, I wanted it. I wanted to be inside of her, and the guilt that accompanied that thought broke my heart.

"Oh, Dylan...you poor, sweet man," she said, the tip of my dick entering her. And all I could think was how much I wished my hands weren't locked up so I could sit her the fuck down. "You'll never understand, will you?"

And finally, the torture stopped, and she rode me, and I watched her tits bounce like a fucking idiot. She held me down with a hand to my chest, the other reaching behind her cowgirl style. I knew I should close my eyes, maybe do my best to picture Alisha's face instead, but I couldn't stop watching her.

I couldn't.

I'd never entertained the thought of a threesome with my

wife, but in that moment, I wanted nothing more than to see her walk through the door and sit on my face.

I relaxed beneath the beautiful lunatic before bucking my hips and driving deeper into her. She squealed, and we were back to fucking just like we used to, *before* she decided she'd rather have my brother.

A small part of me still expected Alisha to come out and yell, "Surprise!"

I had no clue what Ivy's end game was, but I was in it, nonetheless. She'd won, and if all I had to do was fuck her and get it over with, then that's what I was going to do.

"Get off, I'm about to cum," I said through gritted teeth. But she didn't get off, she only rode me harder. "GET OFF!" I screamed, but still, she didn't move, and there was nothing I could do to stop it from happening.

I filled her with all of me, with everything I had to offer, and the shame hit me harder than a tidal wave. "What the fuck is wrong with you?"

Ivy smirked, her eyes rolling to the back of her head. I felt her tighten around my cock, all the while looking me in the eye as she brought herself to orgasm.

And I couldn't help it. The next thing I did was ask if she was still on birth control.

"There's no need to worry about that, Dylan," she said, climbing off me and sauntering slowly to the bathroom. I even watched her walk away. She came out a few minutes later, fully clothed in black leggings and a dark sweatshirt, the hood pulled up over her head and a washcloth in her hands.

"What are you doing?"

She winked, but said nothing, just leaned in and kissed me deeply before pulling away.

And then I saw something in her hand—shiny and...*is that a knife?* I was about to scream as the blade slid into my chest and a spike of pain coursed through my body, sucking the air right from my lungs.

She struggled to pull it out, but managed, only to drive it in a second time.

And a third.

And a fourth...

Until it was dark, and I could no longer breathe because my lungs had filled with blood.

Her face was blurry—almost like an illusion as she faded away.

But her face isn't the last I see.

Alisha, sweetie, I'm so sorry.

My love.

EVEN IN DEATH

Alisha

I RETURNED from my run to find the door off the kitchen slightly open. I couldn't remember locking it, so it was possible it had blown open from the wind. That, or we had an unwelcome rodent roaming the house.

I entered, and this time I locked the door behind me, grabbing my cell off the counter where I left it charging. I'd forgotten to plug it in after my argument with Dylan the night before, so it had run out of battery.

My music-less run did little to clear my head. The note I left him was still on the counter, so I crumpled it up and tossed it in the kitchen trash.

It wouldn't have killed you to tell the truth.

A small part of me was relieved he hadn't seen it. But if Dylan was still asleep, he was sure to be late for work, because I didn't even hear him moving around upstairs. *Maybe he decided to take the day off.*

We did have a lot to talk about. Decisions to consider, apologies to make. And while I was still angry about what I'd learned, the secrets he'd kept from me all that time, I'd realized none of that changed the fact that I loved him. I believed he loved me too, and would do his best to prove it to me every day forward.

His admission hit me hard, but we would be okay. Everything would work out, and we'd be back to normal in no time. The makeup sex was sure to blow my mind—probably his, too.

"Dylan?" I called. "Are you up?"

No answer.

I made my way up the stairs, surprised to find the bedroom door cracked open. I was certain I closed it all the way; I didn't want him to wake before the alarm went off.

"Babe?"

I pressed my hand flat against the door and used my fingers to push it the rest of the way open. My breath caught in my throat when the smell hit me and I gasped, bringing a hand to my mouth.

The sight of him on the bed brought bile to the back of my throat. It bubbled up, despite my attempts to hold it down, and I ran to the bathroom to be sick. I retched, the muscles in my stomach contracting and leaving me breathless. I wiped my mouth on the back of my hand, chunks of vomit still floating around inside.

I didn't want to go back in there.

There was so much blood.

The copper scent clung to my nostrils and made me want to vomit all over again.

I shouldn't have gone back in there.

I stared at his mutilated body from the bathroom floor, the rising sunlight peeking through the windows and reflecting in the exposed metal of the knife that was sticking out of his chest. The cornucopia of colors seemed out of place with its surroundings.

It didn't look right.

And I couldn't stop myself from going to him. I wanted to take his hand, to feel his fingers between mine one last time. I needed to hold him before he went cold.

For a moment, I stood over him, staring as if paralyzed, somehow suspended in time.

When the feeling passed, I lunged forward, wrapping my fingers around the handle of the knife and pulling with every muscle in me. I didn't want it to be in his body. I couldn't stand to see it there, taunting me. I didn't want to see him that way, to remember my husband as a lifeless corpse.

With the knife out, I pulled the white sheet over his torso.

The blood seeped through the fabric, the Egyptian cotton surely ruined. Why that thought crossed my mind, I wasn't sure—it was just a sheet. I could replace it.

But not Dylan.

I reached out and touched his face, my fingers grazing the stubble along his chin. I knew he couldn't feel it, but I took his hand in mine, leaving a kiss on his forehead. His skin was still warm, yet already cold, too.

He was lifeless.

But he was still that same beautiful soul I'd fallen in love with by nothing short of happenstance. And he was beautiful, even in death.

The pounding on the door startled me. I didn't know who it could at that hour, but the shouting came next. I think it surprised me even more than the pounding.

"Police, open up!"

Because how did they already know?

I didn't want to open the door. I didn't want to leave

Dylan, and I couldn't answer any of their questions, because I didn't fucking know what happened to my husband.

So, I froze.

I stood there, at my husband's side, covered in his blood and tightly gripping the knife that had been used to kill him, that I'd later learn had been driven in and out of his flesh a total of seventeen times.

Ironically, the same age I was when my mother died.

The same day of the month Mrs. Maylen left us.

The same number of times I slept with Lila and Grant.

I recognized the knife from the wood block in our kitchen. Even if I hadn't been holding it at that moment, my fingerprints would've been all over it, despite the fact that I rarely cooked.

Fear never settled in.

Not when the officers kicked down my front door.

Not when they stormed through my house.

Not when they pointed their service weapons at my face.

Not even when they cuffed me and read me my Miranda rights.

There was no fear left to be had.

Because everything I was afraid of losing was already gone.

GROW A PAIR, CINDERELLA

Alisha

I COUNT the divots in the bricks on the wall.

One.

Two.

Three.

There's nothing else to do while I await sentencing for the crime I didn't commit. It's been six days since my trial ended, since the verdict was read, my fate decided and publicly announced. Six days since I've done anything other than lie by myself in the confines of my cell, back in the very penitentiary I swore never to return to.

I wasn't supposed to come back here.

And now that I have? It's worse than before. It seems like everyone here is prepared to eat me alive, Officer Marshall included. I've been sent back to the same pod, the same COs overlooking the unit.

A lone enemy in a sea of allies.

So, for now, I stick to my cell, where I can wallow in my misfortune privately. I wallow, and I sleep, and I think. My mind is a constant loop of memories and what ifs and everything in between.

I can't stop thinking about her, about Lila. Wondering how she did it. How she managed to pull off a setup like this. For some reason, that matters more to me than understanding *why*.

I couldn't give a fuck *why* she did it. That knowledge doesn't change the fact that she did. It doesn't change the fact that I'm here. That I'll probably never live beyond the confines of this prison ever again.

I just want to understand how she did it.

She had to have been following me for some time, much longer than I realized. Studying me. Watching Dylan. It had been so long since I'd seen her loitering around the places I frequented, so long since I'd heard from her. But it makes sense in a way, I suppose.

She was always there, I just couldn't see her.

Lila lost her husband; he left her, so in her mind, I had to lose mine too.

Only it doesn't add up. It was me she claimed to love, not Dylan. Not Grant—er, Sawyer. So why not kill me instead? How does killing Dylan and framing me for his murder make everything right for her?

I can't help but wonder if perhaps I wasn't meant to go down for it. Maybe she didn't know I'd come back to the house, that I'd walk into that room and pick up the knife. Maybe she planned to find me afterward and force me to run away with her.

I don't know anymore.

I'm grasping at straws here.

But I have all the time in the world to sit around and think about it, so that's what I do.

"You just gonna rot in there forever, Thompson?" Tiffany asks, rapping her knuckles on the open bars of my cell. I haven't moved from the bed and can't say I plan to. Rec time be damned.

"Yep."

"It doesn't have to be so bad, you know," she says. I can see it in her eyes, that she wants to touch me, maybe put a hand on my arm or something. As if it would offer me comfort.

I already know it won't.

And I sure as shit don't want her touching me.

"Yes, it does," I say. She scoffs, not liking my attitude.

"Oh, grow a pair, Cinderella." She drops to half her size, leaning over with her elbows on her knees, her face inches from mine. Her breath stinks, and I resist the urge to pull away because that's what she wants. "Accepting it is the only way to get back at whoever did this to you."

She shoves off and disappears down the hall, not another word spoken between us. I still don't know if the story she fed me was true, whether she murdered her husband.

Part of me still believes it is, but I'm not about to chase her down, as I'd hate to give her the impression that we're friends.

But once again, she's left me with more insightful words to ponder, and now I'm more annoyed than I was before she stopped in to chat.

Too bad I have no fucking clue what the hell she meant by it.

I'm still pondering it forty minutes later when I'm blessed

with another visitor. "You've got mail, Thompson," CO Marin announces. She pulls the mail cart toward the door and passes me a clipboard. I sign my name with the attached pen and take the envelope from her.

It's another letter from my father.

I toss it onto the stack with the others, plagued with a lack of desire to open it. I can't bring myself to read them yet haven't asked to have him removed from my mailing list either. I haven't decided what I want to do about him.

Instead, I pull out a notebook and pencil, and decide to write a letter to Chris.

I never got to see him in court when the verdict was read, but he was there, standing in the back of the room crying, and ducking out early so he wouldn't have to see me hauled away again.

Dear Chris,

I can't believe you left the sunshine state to come visit me all the way back in Minne-snow-duh—if only I could have seen you, too. I'm sorry I wasn't able to make the wedding, but as you know, it's kinda tough to get out of the office these days.

To be honest, I'm not sure if you even care to hear from me, but I'm writing to you anyway. It brings me comfort to feel like I'm talking to another human, and while you know I hate sappy ass emotions, I owe this to you. I want you to know that I'm okay. That you're the best friend I've ever had.

Oh, quit crying, you big baby…I'll be fine. And I'll understand if having a convicted murderer for a BFF is too much for you…although, who the hell am I kidding? This is some straight-up Real Housewives shit, and you love it.

Thank you for being you, for not giving a shit what

anyone says about me, and for showing up in court. Not just because you had to on account of the subpoena, but because you wanted to show your support. I'm not entirely sure whose story you believe, but I hope that somewhere in your heart, you know the truth.

I'll keep this first letter brief, but I'll write to you again…
Take care, my friend.
Love,
Alisha

P.S. The potatoes here suck. I wish you could smuggle me some. Since you can't, please send me some good books to read.

A KILLER'S TEARS

Alisha

IT'S KINDA FUNNY, isn't it? How deep down you thought I did it. That I killed my husband. It's okay, I'm not mad, it's what I expected of you from the beginning. Like I told you before, the evidence was against me. Hell, I probably would have believed it, too, had I been in your shoes.

Lila made sure to secure the nail in my coffin just as surely as she did Dylan's. We didn't stand a chance once she sunk her teeth in, once she set her sights on destroying us.

And he knew all along.

He could have stopped it.

But he didn't. The lie was just too big.

I miss him every single day. A heavy brick has taken the place of my heart, resting in my chest like a tumor since the moment I found my husband stabbed to death. Since I found him mutilated on our bed. But tears won't bring him back. I know this. I learned that the hard way back when I realized my mother was too far gone to ever come back.

I was reminded of it when I lost Mrs. Maylen.

Everyone I love dies.

See, that's why it really doesn't matter that I'm here for the long haul. As I said before, there's nothing left out there for me. The irony is that I've been here all this time for the wrong reasons—for the wrong murder. And maybe that doesn't matter, maybe this is where I was always supposed to be. Statistics favor such an argument, if you think about it.

Absent father.

Drug-abusing mother.

Poverty.

Sex addiction.

The cards were stacked against me since the day I was born, my fate sealed the second my mother decided not to abort me.

"My little tax deduction," she used to say. Until I was old enough to know better, it always made me smile when she'd call me that, like the child in me thought it was a term of endearment or something.

Childhood made me hard. These walls I keep up were erected a long time ago, built of concrete—of brick and mortar—and meant to withstand the tests of time.

They're unbreakable now.

But the misconception of a heart protected by concrete is that it never had room to love. It's hard for a jury to believe your story when you're labeled as heartless and—how did they say it? Oh, yes. *A sex-crazed lunatic.* Kyle says I should have cried in court, that I should have shown more emotion during the trial.

I wasn't sure how to do that when everything I've ever loved is gone.

Taken from me.

Prematurely stripped from my life.

Erased like a white board.

You see, my love, it never mattered who killed you. There will never be justice, or even closure. Nothing has mattered since I lost you.

Nothing.

There will be no life on the outside for me after this, even if I'm paroled down the road. Kyle wants to file an appeal, now that he finally believes in my innocence. I'm not entirely sure what changed his mind, but something did, and I guess that's good enough for me.

At least *someone* believes me.

But there's no point in being out there without you.

I'm done fighting. I'm tired.

So, my love, that's why—although I know you won't agree with my logic—it's time for me to earn my stripes. To live up to the sentence that was given to me by performing the very act I was convicted of, the crime that put me here.

Murder.

I can't stand the idea of living out the rest of my life in here otherwise.

I see him approaching, rounding the corner like he's on a mission. It's too late to turn and run—the others are already clearing the hall, migrating to their watch posts, readying themselves for the live show.

He's come for me again.

"I wish I could see you in one of your outfits," he growls into my ear as he shoves me against the wall. His arousal digs into my hip, his tongue slick as it trails along my earlobe. His breath is hot on my face, frantic. His excitement builds quickly, more so than usual, and he runs his hands up my thigh, pushing greedily between my legs.

But today I don't give him the win.

I don't relax and pretend he's Dylan, I don't give him the satisfaction he's come for. Today we're going to sing a different song, play a different game.

"Spread 'em," he says into my neck, his hands suddenly rough when he realizes I'm putting up a fight.

I shove against him, pushing off the wall for momentum and knocking him backward. He stumbles, and it's just enough leeway for me to slide the makeshift weapon from my pocket. I turn before he has a chance to realize what's happening, and drive the point of the shiv into his carotid artery.

I pull it out and jam it in once more.

Then again.

His eyes bulge, and he brings his hands to his neck, trying to cover the holes, as if he can stop the blood from pouring out. He opens his mouth and tries to speak, but the words don't follow, just the sound of him gurgling. I smile, my eyes locked on his, watching while he stumbles backward, the color already draining from his face. The blood is everywhere, pooling at my feet, and soaking into my uniform.

This time, it doesn't make me sick.

This time, it's absolutely fucking beautiful.

I exhale heavily, relief coursing through my veins, and I slide down the wall and onto the floor, my hand landing in the crimson puddle beside me. I relax against the wall, my leg now draped over his, and watch in a daze as the motion in his chest finally stops.

A rogue tear rolls down my blood-stained cheek, and I swipe it away before the cavalry arrives and finds me whimpering like a child. But Tiffany is there, leaning nonchalantly against the wall, a sadistic smile playing on her lips.

"A killer's tears bring no mercy," she says.

She leans down and kisses my forehead, taking the blood-soaked shiv from my hand and sliding it into her pocket. I had to give her a taste just to agree to let me use it, but an orgasm is a small price to pay in exchange for one's sanity.

The security alarm sounds above us, the shrilling blast deafening, but I tune it out and close my eyes. Sometimes you have to set the alarm bells ringing just to turn down the noise.

LIKE A BIRD IN FLIGHT

Ivy/Lila

ALISHA, Alisha, Alisha…how dare you do what you've done to me.

To *us*.

You truly do deserve everything that's come your way, don't you? It does pain me a bit to think that—to say it—but our true colors do tend come out in the wash. Certainly you should know this by now.

Sex has been your weapon your entire life, like a nuclear bomb sure to explode at any moment. But it won't work for you anymore, my love.

Not.

Anymore.

People like you are users. Maybe not of drugs, but certainly of other people, and that's the worst kind if you ask me. You use people to get what you want. You prey on women like me.

We are the weaker sex, after all, right? Isn't that what makes it so easy? I really should have seen it coming, that you'd shatter this fragile thing we built together. So carelessly, too.

Imagine that, huh? Well, I'm tired of being ignored. Of being shoved to the back burner because I was never good enough for top choice. But you had no problem holding on until someone better came along. Until *he* got in the way. And what about me? Who was I supposed to get in the end?

Certainly not Sawyer.

Not even you.

I loved you, you know. I loved my husband, too. But you took him from me. You ripped his love for me straight out of his chest and kept it all for yourself. And the worst part is, you didn't even need him. You already had your person, Alisha. You had Dylan.

Why the fuck did you have to take Sawyer, too?

I warned him you would do this. That you'd leave us. That idiot was so pigheaded, he refused to believe me. Until he saw you with *him*.

His own fucking brother.

And it made sense, really. Of course it did. An eye for an eye. Tit for fucking tat. But you know what? *Our* story was supposed to be different. It wasn't just about Dylan catching Sawyer and me in the act all those years ago. The truth is, I simply didn't love him anymore. He practically pushed me into Sawyer's arms when he chose his career over me. So don't go feeling sorry for him.

The heart wants what it wants, right?

Our real problems started after Dylan made you shut down *Lisha's Bedroom*. He always was a coward, never did have much of a backbone. Your dear husband wasn't as wonderful and perfect as you made him out to be. He didn't even have the decency to be honest with you—not even *after* he talked you into marrying him.

And who do you suppose had to make up for what Sawyer lost after your channel went down?

He made me dress like you. Made me wear a wig the same shade as your hair, the same length, the same style. I did my makeup like yours, stuffed my bra so my breasts would look bigger—like yours. But the worst part of it all—the thing that broke me—is that he made me answer to your name. Lila was gone, her persona no longer in service. No longer of use to him.

And Ivy? Ha! She—*I*—died long before Lila was born.

Even as you, I wasn't good enough for him. He knew I was a fake, a stand in. So, what did I have left in the end? My husband certainly didn't need me anymore, didn't want me. He wanted *you*. So it looks like that left me with no one.

Poor Ivy draws the short end of the stick once again.

That's why I had no choice but to seek you out. Why I tracked you and followed your daily schedule, ended up in the same places at the same time. Did you really forget that I don't like coffee? That shit is disgusting. Seriously, I don't know how you drink it. Anyway, I studied you, your mannerisms, your moves. I honestly couldn't figure out what was so special about you that I didn't have. What I was completely blind to was that you were just *you*. Some magical fucking creature; a rainbow-colored unicorn in a field of white horses.

And damn it, I wanted my unicorn back.

I fell for you in the process of losing Sawyer.

And I wasn't about to lose you too.

We could have been so good together, you and me. Even with Sawyer as the third wheel. Even if he wasn't around at all. I could live without the dick if I meant we could be together. Could you?

I suppose you have to now, being in a women's prison and all. It kinda makes me laugh a little bit inside, the thought of you in there with no one to take care of your needs.

You poor thing.

It's really too bad Dylan had to die. It's not like I hated him; there just wasn't room for him with what I had planned for us. You know he never would have accepted me into your bed, and that just wouldn't have been fair. He was nothing like his brother, and unlike Sawyer, Dylan never would have shared his most prized possession.

I had to show you, Alisha. I needed you to understand what you've done to me, how you've changed me, what you've taken from me. I needed *you* to change, too. To feel the same gut-wrenching pain I've felt every day since I first caught Sawyer watching your fucking website. Since the day he chose you over me.

Since *you* ruined him. See, you're not so innocent in all this either.

At least now I know neither of them can stick their dicks in you anymore. Thank God, because the thought of you fucking someone other than me at this point? It makes my damn stomach hurt. Jealousy does run thicker than water, you know.

So, here we are, my love. It's you and me now. I know you don't see it that way, but you will. You'll need a friend to visit you in that hell-hole soon, to put money in your commissary and write to you from the outside. I'm sending this first letter today, in fact, and I've enclosed a photo of me that you'll be able to tape up on the wall next to your government-issued bed. I'll send the racier ones your way once you prove to me that you deserve them.

And you will.

You'll see.

Of course, I have a photo of you next to my bed, too. Sometimes it helps me sleep at night, seeing your beautiful face. You were supposed to be here, sleeping next to me.

But that mistake is on you, not me.

Anyway, you're probably a little confused about the second photo I've enclosed.

The bump is really starting to show, and I can't wait for you to see it, what Dylan and I created together. I wonder how often you think about the fact that I had him last. How he died with the taste of me on his lips.

Does that upset you?

I know it's hard to see in the sonogram, but we're having a boy. I'm sure you'd never deny Dylan's son a chance to see his other mother, would you? I imagine you'd like to watch him grow up, to see whether or not he looks like his father. I'm thinking I may even give him the Thompson name, that way he'll be a part of all of us.

Dylan Sawyer Thompson.

It sure has a nice ring to it, don't you think?

I know one day that boy will be my ticket back to you.

And together?

Well, we'll soar like a bird in flight.

ACKNOWLEDGMENTS

Oh, hey there! You're still with me, huh? Are you over there shouting, "WHAT JUST HAPPENED?" and getting ready to send me an email demanding a sequel? If so, well, this is awkward.

I don't have plans for a sequel…oh, wait. Just kidding, that was in regard to a different book, silly me! There *will* be a sequel for this one, yep. When? Not sure. But maybe (probably) in the near-ish future. Lila/Ivy is still working her way into my head space, but…in time, my dear friend. In time.

With that out of the way, let's proceed with a couple fun facts, shall we? I started writing *Wouldn't You Love to Love Her* a couple years ago while editing my debut, *My Only Sunshine*. I have no idea where the idea stemmed from, or how it shaped into what it is today. But Alisha's character came to life quickly, and in the first week, I managed to write about 15,000 words. Considering my first novel took me thirteen years to write, this was quite unexpected. The project, however, was put on hold. It didn't feel right for this book to follow *My Only Sunshine*, so I took a step back and decided to write something else, something a little more neutral for a transition from contemporary fiction to a psychological thriller like this one. And that resulted in the birth of my sophomore novel, *Even Though It's Breaking*.

Second fun fact: this story was originally titled *A Killer's Tears*, and even had a cover designed with the help of the late Jeremy Whitcomb. While I loved the title and the original cover, as the story came together, it didn't quite feel right. But I did find a way to include the original title in the book; you'll notice it's used as a chapter title in Alisha's final scene.

Third fun fact: the original manuscript only had one narrator, Alisha. Dylan's POV was added later, after seeing how well-received Owen Riverson's character was in *Even Though It's Breaking*.

Last fun fact (are these even interesting?): all my books have chapter titles; however, this is the first time I've included titles in the published copy.

Anyway, I admit, this book was…different? More so than anything I've ever written. It was a bit out of my comfort zone, if I'm being honest, and these characters really challenged me. I kept them at bay for quite some time, and it's nice to finally give them life and introduce them to readers. I am, however, a little concerned about my internet search history—the research on this one was…interesting.

These characters didn't come to life entirely on their own, and for that reason, I have a few people I'd like to thank.

To my family, thank you for giving me the space to focus on my writing. I know it's not always fun, but your continued support of my work means the world to me.

To my editor, Kiezha Ferrell, whom I've now had the opportunity to work with three times, I've said it before, and I'll say it again—you're the best. As always, your perspective and meticulous eye for detail continue to make me a better writer. I'm so honored to have the pleasure of working with you!

To my incredible team of beta readers: Sawyer Cole Hobson, Danielle Renee, Erika Bucci, and Chris Shaneck. Your feedback and willingness to pick apart my manuscript has brought this story to a whole new level. Thank you for your honesty, encouragement, and discretion!

Thank you to the bookstagrammers who allowed me to borrow their names for this story! Sawyer Cole @colesbooknook, Chris @analyzedbychris, Danielle Renee @dani.reads.1225, Lexy @lexy_attemptedmystery (your obsession for Owen Riverson is greatly appreciated!), and Jen @inkdrinkerjen.

To the friends and family whose names I borrowed without permission and sprinkled throughout this book: Sara, (and Teddy!), Amy, Josh, Kristin, Cindy, Lindsay, and for some reason, my third-grade teacher, Mrs. Ronzon—wherever she may be these days. I hope you all enjoyed seeing your names in a book!

And, of course, a special thank you to the most adorable blonde leprechaun, Alisha (@alishareadsgoodbooks), who literally demanded I name the main character after her. I'm low-key still attached to the original character name, but at least I know I'll be able to hold this over her head from now until forever.

To my Jump Street Team, and everyone out there helping me spread the word about my books, you continue to amaze me and I'm so grateful for you! THANK YOU for all you do in support of my craft!

And lastly, to the readers far and wide, whether you loved this book or hated it, thank you for picking it up and giving it a chance.

The *Crimes of Passion* series continues!

The best of two worlds collide in book two of this intensely provocative and addicting psychological thriller series. Full of steam *and* scream, seduction, and deception, the *Crimes of Passion* series is fast-paced, witty, and sure to leave readers on the edge of their seats.

Coming Soon:

LIKE A BIRD IN FLIGHT

ABOUT THE AUTHOR

Shannon Jump is an avid reader and writer, with a passion for storytelling. She refuses to start the day without the perfect cup of coffee and is a die-hard Minnesota Twins baseball fan and Food Network junkie. She lives in small-town Minnesota with her husband and two teenage kids.

If you enjoyed this book, please consider leaving a review, even just a sentence or two will do. Who knows? Your review could be the reason a future reader says "yes" to one of my books! To sign up for my newsletter, shop official merchandise, or stay up to date on my projects, visit my website at https://www.shannonjumpwritesbooks.com.

Looking for another captivating book to read? Be sure to check out my other books, too!

instagram.com/sjump4203

amazon.com/author/shannonjumpbooks

goodreads.com/sjump4203

bookbub.com/profile/shannon-jump

Made in United States
North Haven, CT
05 March 2022

16827654R00153